All the Guns and Whistles

KATY LEE

All the Guns and Whistles
Katy Lee

Book Cover by 100 Covers

Print ISBN: 979-8-9935801-5-9

Printed in the United States of America

"A gift in secret pacifies anger, and a bribe behind the back, strong wrath."

— PROVERBS 21:14

To my daughter Brianna: so thankful you found your home with us.

One

Jayda Simone always carried her pink bedazzled stun gun —she just never thought she would have to use it in Yale's law library. Lately, coffee was her weapon of choice, and after three years of law school, she'd come armed with a tumbler full to tackle a night of studying for her last final—criminal law—the test that had the potential to kill her more than the guy she zapped. Her stun gun wasn't supposed to come out, but the guy in the stacks dressed in black was stealing the file she needed. He gave her no choice. She wouldn't let anyone stand in her way of passing this exam.

Even if he had a gun.

It had been a typical wintry December day. Jayda had trudged through the snow that covered the courtyard and made her way up the steps to Yale's Sterling Memorial Library —a towering gothic castle. Inside, her boots clicked along the marble floor like war drums. Anyone looking at her saw only a polished law student with a chic hair twist that commandeered her black curls. They saw a young woman with her head held high and sporting a smart winter coat.

But the truth?

Jayda was an impostor.

She never understood why Yale had said yes to a girl from the New Haven streets and figured eventually someone would find her out. She hadn't grown up in libraries, hadn't had winter coats that weren't three sizes too big until she was fourteen, and only started drinking coffee when she realized it helped her stay awake in foster homes where locks on bedroom doors were optional. Hence the stun gun—you can take the girl off the streets, but the street smarts never die.

Unbeknownst to the man awaiting her, she had rubbed her weary eyes and tried not to stumble into the elevator to head up to the quiet law stacks. The lights were dimmed when she'd entered the deeper shelves—only making her sleepier for the task ahead—and she had muttered, "Here lies Jayda Simone. Survived the New Haven gangs but slain by criminal procedure."

Jayda never wanted to be a criminal lawyer. Definitely not. She'd seen enough criminals up close. What she wanted was family law, a nice safe courtroom where she could help kids find better outcomes than hers. But Criminal Law was a required class for her degree, and this final exam would determine whether she'd graduate with honors. It would determine her future at a reputable law firm.

She had to ace this test.

Jayda downed another swig of her fuel and had headed to the old case files where Professor Dandridge said they'd be—buried in the annex behind the dusty *Federal Reporter* volumes. He had told the class this case was back in the headlines because the convict was due to be released from prison after thirty years. One of Dandridge's earliest cases, *People v. Langston,* was about a woman who'd vanished after turning state's evidence and was rumored to have entered witness protection. It had nothing to do with family law, but Jayda had always wondered what it would be like to disappear and start over.

The thought had made her smile...still completely unaware of what awaited her right around the corner.

She took the turn and froze.

The thief was dressed in black. Tall, broad, and in an expensive leather coat. She had caught him rifling through the locked filing cabinet—the one she needed. At the sight of his hurried movements, Jayda had known he didn't belong. This section was for students only, and she had never seen him before.

Jayda's instincts had flared. She knew a bad vibe when she felt one. The scar on his cheek looked like it had come from a run-in with a knife.

"Hey," she had said, voice firm. "You're not supposed to be in here."

The man had stiffened but didn't turn. Instead, he slid a thick file into the inside of his coat like it was his birthright. Jayda had stepped closer.

"Those don't leave the library. I'm calling security."

That's when he'd turned.

His face—pale, sharp, and carved from stone—held the look Jayda had seen once before in a man who beat his foster kids and got away with it for years. Cold. Calculating. Dangerous.

"I said," Jayda had repeated, louder now, "put it back."

He'd moved toward her. Fast. So fast that his coat opened, sending the file to the floor, papers flying like the squalling snow outside.

That's when she'd seen the gun.

And him reach for it.

Jayda had dropped her tumbler on the floor. Her fingers dove into her coat. Not for her phone. She wasn't that dumb. Phones didn't stop guns.

But her pink stun gun would...and did. It had stopped him cold. Or more like a heated bolt of lightning Jayda hadn't thought. With one hand she'd pressed the button, the other, she'd used to slam the stun gun against his side. The click-click-zap filled the air, and so did his scream. A terrifying howl of pain and rage as his body jerked violently before her.

She stunned someone.

And now all she could do was wonder how this had happened.

Jayda stood face to face with the man, trembling in shock as she watched him drop to the floor and writhe...all because of her.

Heart thudding, she turned with a pivot to retreat, wondering if her life would always be a fight to survive.

Jayda couldn't wait to find out.

But before she ran, a glossy photo caught her eye midstride. There, among the mess from the spilled file, was a picture of a woman. Pretty. Late twenties. Boarding a train.

Something about her face struck Jayda. Not just her expression—but the fear in her eyes.

Was this the woman the man had come for?

Without thinking, Jayda grabbed the photo and a few scattered documents. Another photo of the woman was beneath the papers, and Jayda took it too and ran again for the stairs.

Her phone buzzed in her purse. She yanked it out, hoping to call the police, but the screen showed the caller: *Ginny Blair*.

Jayda groaned.

Foster mom #4. Christmas-crazy. Holiday obsessed. And the closest thing Jayda ever had to a mom after her birth mom died.

Not now, Ginny.

Jayda ignored the call, heart pounding. She barreled down

the stairs. First floor in sight. She swung the door wide and burst out just as the elevator dinged ten feet away.

The elevator opened. The man stepped out. Limping. Gun now in his hand.

He didn't see her but scanned the crowd.

Jayda took cover and ducked behind a pillar, then sprinted for the exit.

Where was security? She passed the check-in desk—empty. The security guard was probably in the breakroom having a snack. Figures when they are needed most.

She reached the front doors. Daylight. Almost safe. She looked back—he'd spotted her, limping her way.

"Gun!" she yelled and raced outside and down the steps.

Jayda ran harder, away from the chaos she stirred up behind her, needing to put distance between her and the man. She could only hope he'd been stopped or derailed from chasing her.

Her phone rang. Ginny again. Anyone but Ginny, but that's all Jayda had to work with. At least if the man caught up with her, Ginny would be on the phone.

Jayda answered purely out of selfishness. "Ginny!" she panted as she ran and looked over her shoulder across the snow-laden courtyard. At any other time, the sight would be postcard-worthy.

"Jayda? Are you all right?" Ginny's chipper voice rang in her ear. "Are you crying? Oh, honey, you sound so upset—"

"I'm not,"—she panted— "not crying—running."

"Running? Where? Oh, never mind. Listen. I just wanted to tell you about the twins we started fostering last month—four years old, both of them, and I swear I'm going gray. Oh, what a handful! And—"

"Ginny. Not a good time."

"Well, when is it a good time with you, huh? You never come home anymore. Which is why I called. We're having a holiday reunion. The whole family is getting together for the entire week. They would love to see you. And so would I. We're all so proud of you and all you've accomplished. Will you come?"

Jayda skidded around a corner and slipped into the alley behind the next building. No sign of the man. Had she lost him?

She leaned against a brick wall, catching her breath.

Ginny kept talking. "It'll be magical! We'll bake cookies and decorate gingerbread houses. And of course there'll be presents. I think I still have your gifts from last year, so you'll get double."

Jayda looked down at the photos still in her hand. The woman stood on the famous crooked street in San Francisco. In the second picture, she stepped onto a train.

Jayda made a snap decision.

"Sorry, Ginny. I can't come. I'm going on a cross-country trip. San Francisco." *Maybe even out of the country if that's not far enough.*

"San Fran! Maybe we can join you!"

A glance at the second picture gave Jayda the perfect out. "I'm traveling by train," she added. How long *was* the cross-country train ride? A week? Two? Too long for Ginny and four-year-old twins, that was for sure.

"*What*? Oh, that's perfect! We'll all go with you! What fun! I've always wanted to see the Rockies by train."

Jayda peered around the corner of the building. "No, Ginny, you—"

"Don't worry. I'll plan it all. The whole family—Michael too."

"Michael?" Her voice squeaked. "That isn't—"

"He'll get the time off. I'm calling him right now."

"Ginny, please don't—"

The line went dead.

"Ginny?" Jayda blinked at her phone. *What had just happened*? In running from a killer, Jayda had instead been ambushed by Ginny. Jayda groaned, slid down the alley wall, and let her head *clunk* gently against the bricks.

"I should've let the killer shoot me."

I can't go to San Francisco.

I can't be stuck on a train with the Blair family and their new foster kids. With Michael!

What have I done?

By the time Jayda had slunk home to graduate housing and shut the door of her apartment behind her, twenty minutes had passed, and her phone had buzzed five times. Three missed calls and two texts.

All were from Michael Blair.

~

Michael Blair's article was good.

Scratch that—it was more than good. It was sharp, thorough, and relevant, the in-depth political analysis *The New York News* was supposed to champion.

But his boss, Harold McKenna, was tearing it apart like it was a bad first draft from a freshman journalism student.

"I don't care if it's airtight, Michael," Harold said, waving a hand at the computer screen where Michael's article was pulled up. Harold acted as if the words offended him. "It's about conflict in the Middle East. Conflict is depressing. We're going into Christmas, and no one wants depressing."

Michael, seated across from him, leaned forward. "It's not depressing. It's important. It's about how fragile the peace talks—"

Harold held up a hand. "Our readers want Christmas cheer. Hope. Nostalgia. Something they can sip cocoa over while the tree lights twinkle. You've been here long enough to know the drill."

Michael blinked. "You're rejecting it? Just like that?"

"Yes. Just like that."

Michael pinched the bridge of his nose. "So instead of covering one of the most important geopolitical stories of the year, you want me to...what? Write about sugar cookies?"

"Not cookies," Harold said, leaning back in his chair. "Something big. Festive. Human interest." He paused. "You married?"

Michael stared at him. Michael had worked for the man for a year. Did he even know him? "No."

"But you have a family, right?"

"Yes, if you mean my parents...and their foster kids."

Harold's eyes lit up. "Perfect. A real Shirley Temple Christmas. I want you to lean on family. People love family Christmas stories."

Michael opened his mouth to argue, but his phone vibrated in his pocket. He removed it to see his mother's name flash on the screen. Again. He'd been dodging her calls all morning, knowing exactly what she wanted to talk about.

This silly train trip idea she'd conjured up.

He ignored the call. "What exactly do you have in mind, Harold?"

"I don't know. Something that screams Christmas spirit." Harold's gaze sharpened. "What's your family's big holiday plan this year?"

Michael hesitated. He'd told absolutely no one about the absurdity Ginny had concocted that morning. "It's...crazy. Nothing you'd be interested in. And neither am I, for that matter. My mom's dragging everyone on some ridiculous cross-country train trip she's calling 'The Blair Polar Express.'" He made air quotes with his fingers. "I have no intention of going."

Harold sat up so fast his chair squealed against the floor. "A train trip?"

Michael immediately regretted opening his mouth. "Don't get any ideas—"

"That's perfect!" Harold slapped the desk. "Think about it: cross-country, family reunion, foster kids, Christmas décor, snow, strangers stuck together for days—it's nostalgic gold. People eat that stuff up. And you'd be right there, documenting the magic."

Michael stared. "Documenting the magic? Harold, it's my family. There is no magic."

Harold grinned like the devil himself. "Then fake it. Or better yet, write it in a way that makes readers believe in it. You've got less than two weeks until Christmas Eve. I want it on my desk by the twenty-third. We'll run it Christmas morning."

"I'm not going," Michael said flatly.

"Yes, you are. Unless..." Harold's tone shifted, casual but sharp. "...you think you're above this job. I can hire another columnist who will jump at the idea."

Michael stiffened.

Harold didn't break eye contact. "You're welcome to test the waters elsewhere. Lots of outlets are hiring this time of year."

Michael swallowed the retort burning on his tongue. His father's voice echoed in his head, deep and unyielding. *A Blair doesn't quit. A Blair earns respect through work.*

The Honorable Judge Edward Blair would never respect his son walking out over a Christmas assignment.

Michael forced his jaw to unclench. "Fine."

Harold's grin widened. "Knew you'd see reason. Now go pack your snow boots and find the soul of Christmas."

"Yes, sir." Michael left Harold's office deflated, resentment curling in his gut. He grabbed his coat from his desk, needing some fresh air. He couldn't make small talk in the elevator, and when he stepped into the cold December air, Manhattan's Christmas lights mocked him from every lamppost.

Two weeks trapped with his family. Two weeks stuck on a train while pretending to care about ornaments and gingerbread houses. And worst of all—Jayda Simone.

The phone in his pocket was still warm from calling her all morning and from her ignoring his every attempt.

He stopped walking, thumb hovering over her contact. The last time they'd spoken was at least six months ago, and that was only because she'd needed something from his mother. Jayda never called to catch up. Never showed up for holidays unless guilt-tripped. Never expressed gratitude for what the Blairs had done for her.

Ungrateful.

That was the word that always came to mind.

She didn't know the half of what his parents—what *he*—had done to make her life easier. She believed she'd gotten into Yale Law purely on merit. Never guessed about the quiet phone call his father, the judge, made to an old friend on the admissions board. Never guessed that without the Blairs, she'd still be scraping by in some under-funded community college.

Michael hit *Call* to try again.

Three rings. Four. He was about to hang up. But this time, she answered.

"You have to get us out of this," Jayda said. No hello. No preamble.

Michael blinked, caught off guard. "Out of what?"

"This train trip. Tell your mom you can't go."

A laugh escaped him—sharp, amused. "Why? Afraid you'll have to spend time with us?"

"I just..." She hesitated, sounding distracted...nothing new there. "It's complicated. Something's come up."

"It's always complicated with you." He leaned against a

lamppost, letting the winter wind bite his cheeks. "You never wanted to be part of my family, Jayda. But my parents—my *mother*—bent over backwards for you. She still does. You could at least be thankful."

Silence crackled across the line.

Michael pressed on, a smirk tugging at his lips. "You know what? I *am* looking forward to this train ride. Maybe you'll remember how much the Blairs have done for you."

"Michael—"

"I'll see you at Penn Station tomorrow afternoon," he cut in. "Be sure to bring your jingle bells."

Before she could reply, he hung up.

The satisfaction was immediate and petty, exactly the fuel he needed to get through the next two weeks.

If Harold wanted a "Polar Express" story, Michael Blair would give him one. But not the sugar-coated version. No—he'd write the truth. And maybe, just maybe, the people who deserved coal would finally get it.

Two

Jayda stuffed a backpack like she was a fugitive. Which, technically she wasn't, but after introducing twelve thousand volts of electricity into a man with a gun and menacing scar, self-defense skills offered little comfort.

She yanked open her closet and grabbed more items: a thick sweater, a pair of jeans, and—because life was cruel—her last pair of clean socks with tiny candy canes on them. She shoved them into her backpack, ignoring the neat pile of casebooks on her desk, the ones she was supposed to have been reviewing last night for today's criminal law exam. Instead, she stayed up all night on guard in case she had an unwanted visitor.

Thankfully, "Scar" hadn't found out where she lived.

See, Michael? I'm thankful for something.

All night long, Michael's voice rang in her ears from their brief phone call: *You could at least be thankful.*

Her grip tightened on the sweater.

Thankful. For what, exactly? For the years of polite but uncomfortable dinners at the Blair house? For the way Michael always looked at her like she'd stolen a place at the table that didn't belong to her? For being reminded at every opportunity that she was the charity case in a family of over-achievers?

And yet—*ugh*—there was the guilt. A small, irritating, *traitorous* voice in her head whispered that maybe she had been standoffish, maybe Ginny Blair really had meant well, maybe Michael wasn't *entirely* wrong.

Jayda shoved the thought away. She didn't have the capacity for emotional self-examination when she was possibly on a mobster's hit list.

She needed to find out who the guy was.

Her gaze slid to her phone, lying face-down on the desk. She could call the police. She could tell them about the man in the library, about how he chased her with a gun after she'd bolted. She could even give them a decent description—black leather coat, snake tattoo on the neck, scar beneath eyes that said he enjoyed hurting things.

But the idea curdled in her stomach. Growing up in the system had left her with a healthy skepticism of authority. The cops had never been on her side—not when her mother got sick, not when the landlord evicted them from the tiny apartment, not when Child Protective Services showed up two weeks after the funeral to split her from the only neighbors who'd cared.

The cops couldn't protect her now. They'd take a report, maybe run a patrol past the library, and that would be the end.

Meanwhile, Jayda knew that man was coming for her...for the pictures and documents she'd swiped from the floor. Jayda grabbed them and added them to her bailout bag. For whatever reason, he wanted them, and Jayda didn't think it was for reuniting with an old friend.

Who was the woman to him? Was she in danger? In need of protection?

Jayda couldn't worry about her right now. Not when

Jayda's days in family law hadn't started yet—and they wouldn't if she didn't take her final exam. Shaking off the image of the woman in the picture, Jayda's mind returned to the test awaiting her. All the late nights, the lectures she'd forced herself to sit through despite exhaustion, the endless outlines and flashcards—it all came down to this week. If she failed the final, she might as well drop out. Law school didn't forgive that kind of stumble. A poor grade could end her future acceptance at a prestigious law firm. She needed to take the exam, get a good grade, and get out of town.

But to where?

If she didn't get on that train and go west, where else could she go? And if she boarded that train, was she walking right into another fiasco of the Ginny Blair kind?

Jayda grabbed her heaviest winter coat—a puffy black monstrosity that could double as personal body armor—and looped a wool scarf around her neck three times. Then sunglasses. She caught sight of herself in the mirror and almost laughed.

"I look like an incognito snowman," she muttered.

But overkill was better than being killed.

She zipped the coat, slung the backpack over her shoulders, and headed out. Careful to keep her head down, she made her way to her classroom building. Her every step was focused and moving quickly. Her boots shuffled through the fresh snow as she took the sidewalk toward the brick structure ahead. She was almost there...until she reached the bottom of the stairs and looked up.

Three men in dark jackets stood by the front doors, scanning every student who approached. One of them—Scar—took a step forward.

Her heart lurched.

She pivoted hard, pretending to check her phone, then ducked down the side street. She kept walking until she was three blocks away, lungs tight, sweat prickling under her coat despite the cold.

No exam today. No passing grade. No Yale Law degree if she couldn't make this up—and the odds of that happening were slimmer than her chances of winning the lottery.

A sharp, hollow ache filled her chest. She'd worked too hard, sacrificed too much, to lose it all now.

And then the anger came.

Not the hot, reckless kind. The deep molten kind that burned slowly with the old fury of injustice. She knew it well.

It was the same anger she'd felt at eight years old, watching her mother shrink into a hospital bed, knowing the cancer was winning because the system didn't care about people like them. Her mother had worked herself to the bone—two jobs, no insurance—until she simply couldn't anymore.

Jayda watched her mother die and had sworn that one day she'd fight her way back. Law school was supposed to be that way.

She couldn't let a smug mobster take it from her.

She also couldn't let him take her life.

Jayda walked faster, checking over her shoulder every block she made it to...every block that led to New Haven's train station. Car tires sloshed wet snow in her path, slowing down her quick pace. She felt too exposed, waiting to be cut off at every alley. She pushed on with short, determined breaths.

By the time she reached the station, her breath fogged in the cold air and her calves ached from the stride. The station loomed ahead, all glass and stone, and she didn't hesitate. She bought a ticket for the next train—didn't care where it went—then darted down the stairs and the long white tiled corridor to the next departing train's platform. The train doors stood wide, waiting for her.

She dropped into a seat, her backpack clutched tight to her

chest. Only when the train lurched forward did she allow herself to exhale.

The destination scrolled across the overhead screen.

New York City.

Her stomach tightened. Michael—and the rest of the Blairs—would board their ridiculous Polar Express this afternoon, expecting her to join them.

But she was on the run.

Then again, the bad guys would never imagine her walking straight into a family holiday.

Perhaps Jayda could paste on a smile and sing a few songs to make Ginny happy—if it meant she stayed alive.

~

The platform bustled with the usual mix of exciting chatter from arrivals, but for Michael it might as well have been a stage. He pasted on a smile while his family gathered near the car assigned to them, their cluster of luggage stacked with Ginny's usual tidy precision. His father, Ed, stood tall and robust, scanning the crowd like a man still half-expecting something to go wrong. His mother, always chipper, stooped near the twins, fastening the zipper on one boy's jacket while the other darted a few steps away to peek inside the train car.

Michael adjusted the strap of his computer bag over his shoulder and joined them. "You're all looking ready for the grand adventure," he said, letting his voice carry a warmth he didn't entirely feel. He was tired already—travel wasn't leisure for him, not when his mind catalogued every face, every overheard snippet, like notes for a story that might someday matter—and for the one he had to write.

"Michael!" His mother rose and wrapped him in a quick hug. She smelled faintly of her familiar lavender lotion. "I'm so glad you're here. This will be good for you."

He nearly laughed. She said it as though a train ride across the country would reset all his bad habits and sort out the stalled state of his career. But he kissed her cheek anyway and squeezed her shoulder.

Uncle Henry was next—round, genial, with a booming laugh already spilling out as though the mere sight of Michael was comedy enough. Aunt Caroline gave Michael a peck on the cheek, her perfume still as cloying as ever.

And then, standing just a step behind them, was Simon.

Michael hadn't seen his cousin since last Christmas, or was it Thanksgiving? Thirty years old now, Simon Blair was tall and looked like he'd stepped straight from the glossy pages of some lifestyle magazine—tailored coat, scarf knotted carelessly in that perfect I-don't-care way that meant he probably spent ten minutes in the mirror perfecting it. His grin was wide, his teeth blinding, his cologne sharp and expensive. He clasped Michael's hand in a shake that turned into a half-hug as if they were brothers instead of blood-related strangers.

"Cousin," Simon said with theatrical warmth. "Wouldn't miss this for the world."

Michael offered the same grin he might to a source he didn't trust. "Good to see you. I didn't realize you were coming along," he said, careful to keep his tone light.

"Last minute decision. Decided to join in just this morning," Simon said breezily, like he was talking about ordering dessert instead of uprooting to spend days locked in a train car with extended family. "But with Darlene gone, I figured—why not? New scenery. Fresh air. Adventure."

Darlene. The marriage everyone had quietly tiptoed around at holidays was now officially over. Michael raised an eyebrow. "Sorry to hear it. What happened?"

Simon shrugged as if tossing away a coat. "She wanted different things. I wanted freedom. *C'est la vie*, right?"

Nothing more. The topic was dismissed with the smoothness of a politician side-stepping scandal.

Michael nodded slowly but wondered about the truth.

It wasn't just Simon's glossed-over answers that set Michael's reporter instincts buzzing. It was the way Simon moved—casual, confident, as though money cushioned every step. When Ginny passed him his train ticket, he tucked it in his breast pocket, exposing a thick wad of cash. Not a few bills. A wad. Michael doubted Simon even realized he'd revealed it, or maybe he did it on purpose. Some men liked to display power and wealth like cufflinks.

"So, what have you been up to?" Michael braced for the onslaught of stories that would spring forth from Simon's mouth.

His cousin didn't disappoint.

Simon spouted on and on about his recent trip to Morocco, an acquaintance who knew a cabinet minister in Italy, a party in Dubai where he'd met someone whose name Michael recognized from the news. The details always flowed easily from Simon's bragging mouth. But there was always a polish to it all, a too-perfect sheen that kept Michael's instincts on high alert.

Michael let him talk. That's the thing about people like Simon: the more rope given to them, the more likely they are to hang themselves. Still, Michael plastered on a smile, nodding at the right beats, though his inner notebook was already scribbling questions.

Drugs? Smuggling? Some kind of offshore scheme?

"Boys," Ed called, snapping Michael's attention to the twins. They were clambering onto the edge of a piece of luggage, pretending it was a horse. Ginny tried to corral them, exasperation etched in every line of her face. A wisp of her gray hair sprung loose from her low bun and whipped across her face.

"They're spirited," Michael said diplomatically.

"They're four," Ginny replied, tugging one down before he toppled. "Everything is a game at four. They'll be fine once the train moves."

Two sets of identical brown eyes widened. "Will it go fast?" one asked. Timothy or was it Tyler? Michael hadn't spent enough time with them to tell the difference.

"Faster than any horse," Michael promised, and the boys giggled before bolting in different directions again.

Simon leaned in, lowering his voice just enough for Michael to catch the cadence. "They'll exhaust us before we reach Chicago."

Michael smirked, though his mind looped in on Simon's expensive wool coat. His cousin was well-fed, well-traveled, *and* well-dressed. To his family, Simon was the prodigal cousin returned to grace them with his charm. To Michael, he was a question mark dressed in finery.

Michael shoved his suspicions down where they belonged. No sense airing them now, not on the edge of what Ginny clearly hoped would be a bonding journey for the holiday reunion.

"Glad you're here," Michael said aloud to Simon, plastering cheer over his doubt. "This trip just got more interesting." Not a lie. Though Michael didn't think Simon would be the kind of story his boss was looking for either. But he sure would fit an editorial piece on con men among us.

Simon flashed that smile again. He glanced down the platform as though he were looking for someone. "Exactly what I thought. Interesting. This trip should be very interesting."

The twins barreled back toward Michael like pint-sized torpedoes in puffy jackets, mittens flapping, voices high and eager.

"Michael! Michael! Did you bring us presents?" Timothy or Tyler squealed.

"Yeah, presents!" the other echoed, tugging at Michael's coat sleeve with sticky fingers that smelled faintly of candy canes.

Michael crouched down, forcing a smile that came easier than expected. "You know Santa's already got you covered, right? But I did bring some surprises for the ride." He tapped his bag. Their eyes widened as if he'd told them he had the key to Willy Wonka's factory.

"Later," Ginny said firmly, stepping between the boys. She adjusted one boy's hat and straightened the other's scarf with the same mother-hen efficiency she'd once used on Michael and every one of her foster children after him. He'd lost count over the years. "They've already had more sugar than sense today. Save your bribes for when the cabin fever sets in."

Her words were warm, but her eyes held a glint of warning —the look she gave him every time she thought he might cause problems. She saw straight through him. The years hadn't dimmed her intuition. She should have been the reporter in the family. Nothing got past her.

Behind his mother stood his father, his gray wool coat dusted with flurries. He clamped Michael's shoulder in a single squeeze that said what his quiet mouth never did. *I'm glad you're here.*

"Leave it to your mother to plan such a shindig," his dad said.

"Oh, no, this was all Jayda's idea," Ginny replied. "Now where is that child?"

Ginny looked over the boys' heads to the entrance to the platform. Worry etched her brow, and Michael could have kicked Jayda for doing this to his mother. Every year, Jayda blew them off.

Michael didn't mask his I-told-you-so look.

"She'll come," his mother whispered, stopping him from voicing his opinion further.

Michael bit back the retort. Of course, she believed in Jayda. She always had. Even when no one else did, including him.

"She's not coming, Mom," Michael said as sympathetically as possible.

Her hand tightened around her purse strap. She lifted a daring chin and stated, "She'll be here."

"Your confidence in her is misplaced. Always has been."

"I disagree. You'll see."

The conductor's whistle shrieked across the platform. "All aboard!" he called.

The twins squealed with delight. Ginny herded them toward the train, muttering, "Come on, come on. Let's get you settled before you freeze." But her eyes—sharp as ever—scanned the platform behind them before she stepped up the steps, guiding the boys to their seats.

The train lurched with the first groan of movement. Ginny's face pinched, her hand pressing against the glass as she peered out the window of the car.

And then—

"Michael!" she cried, startling everyone. "Michael, help her! She's here! Jayda's here!"

Michael moved to the window, and there she was, barreling down the platform, coat flapping open, curls wild, determination blazing in her eyes. She was late. Of course, she was late. But she was here.

For a moment, the years melted away. She wasn't a Yale Law student, wasn't a woman running to catch a train. She was just the same Jayda who used to beat him at chess and smirk about it for days.

The train picked up speed.

"Go!" Ginny ordered, practically shoving him toward the sliding door to the outside hallway.

Michael grumbled and wondered why he had agreed to

always clean up Jayda's messes, but he still did as his mother ordered.

Outside the car, he swung himself onto the outside steps leaving the platform, one hand gripping the cold metal rail, the other stretched out for her.

"Come on, Jayda!" he shouted.

She lunged, her hand slapping against his, and he hauled her up with more force than finesse. She slammed into him, the momentum driving her against his chest. For one shocking second, their faces stood inches apart, their breath mingled in the cold air.

"You're always late," Michael accused, his voice rougher than he intended.

Jayda's lips curved. "Only when you're around. The less time near you, the better."

The jab was sharp, practiced. She meant it to sting. Same old Jayda, different day.

Michael let her go, turning to retreat inside, pretending the heat in his chest was just from the effort he exerted.

But something made him glance back.

Jayda stood on the landing, her teeth sinking into her lower lip, eyes fixed on the platform. Not on him. Not on Ginny, who waved furiously from behind the door's window.

But on two men dressed head to toe in black, sprinting across the platform where Jayda had just jumped aboard. But they weren't just sprinting.

They were armed.

Each carried a gun, glinting beneath the harsh station lights.

Michael's stomach dropped. He instantly stepped in front of Jayda, his arm up to push her back out of their view.

"Who are they?" he demanded.

Jayda's head whipped toward him, her eyes wide. "Just... people who missed the train."

The words tumbled too fast, too easily. Relief flooded her face as if she'd convinced herself more than him.

"You never could lie with a straight face. You'll make a terrible attorney."

She huffed and slipped past him into the car, not looking back. She let Ginny wrap her up in a welcoming hug as though she were the sweet, innocent daughter they never had.

Michael didn't believe her for a second. What kind of trouble was Jayda in? Obviously, something illegal. As the train pulled away from the platform, leaving the men in black shrinking into the distance, one thought pounded in Michael's head.

His parents could take the girl off the streets, but they could never take the streets out of the girl.

Three

Jayda pasted on the brightest smile she could manage as the Blair family settled around a table in the dining car. The small space bustled with chatter, clinking silverware, and the gentle sway of the train beneath them. The Blairs had commandeered a long table by the window, where the snow-dusted scenery of the Hudson Valley blurred past in streaks of white and gray. Ginny handed everyone their room keys to their private sleeping quarters, two for each in case they lose one. Ginny always planned for the inevitable. Jayda yearned to slip away, but Aunt Caroline reached across the table to squeeze Jayda's hand warmly, her eyes full of excitement, keeping Jayda rooted to her seat.

"Sweet Jayda," Caroline said, almost bursting with delight, "how did finals go? You must feel so relieved to have them behind you."

Jayda's throat tightened. She swallowed against the sudden lump and forced her lips to smile. "Oh, you know...it's a relief, yes." Her voice came out smooth, how she hoped to sound in a courtroom someday. She lifted her teacup like a shield and took a sip before anyone could press too hard for the truth—that she won't be graduating now.

Ed leaned forward, adjusting his glasses on the bridge of his nose. "And the bar exam? You're sitting for it soon, aren't you?" His deep, judicial voice carried a mixture of admiration and expectation.

Jayda curled her fingers tighter around the cup. The truth clawed at her—she'd missed her last final. Missed it because two men in dark coats had cornered her outside the lecture hall. Missed it because she'd been running for her life through city streets instead of writing essays that would lock in her future. And because of that, the bar exam—the finish line she'd worked toward for years—was now out of reach.

She smiled anyway. "I'll be studying on the train," she said lightly. "Plenty of time to cram, right?"

Aunt Caroline beamed. "Perfect! We'll quiz you with flashcards, won't we, Ginny?" She glanced down the table at her sister-in-law.

"You know me. I can't resist," Ginny said, bouncing one boy on her knees. "We'll help Jayda, won't we, boys?"

The boys giggled at the idea, but Jayda's laugh sounded hollow in her ears. "I'd like that," she murmured.

But her mind wasn't on flashcards. It was on the pounding of her shoes against Grand Central's marble floor. The hint of breath on her neck as she sprinted to lose the men outside one station as she ran to another, having no choice but to join the Blairs now. The echo of footsteps had followed her all the way to Penn Station. She glanced toward the window, pretending to admire the snow, when really, she was searching the car for any sign of the men, just in case they had managed to jump on the train.

Across the table, Michael lounged back in his chair, arms crossed, a determined expression in his startling blue eyes. He had seen the men. And he saw straight through her. Always had.

The others laughed and chatted, caught up in reminiscing about past holiday memories, but Michael's gaze never left her. When the noise at the table swelled and attention shifted away, he leaned close, his words pitched just for her.

"You're not fooling me," he murmured. His tone wasn't cruel—just steady, edged with that old mix of irritation and protectiveness he'd worn since they were teenagers—protective of his family, not her. "Who are they?"

"Who?" She practiced her rebuttal face, giving nothing away, and picked up her cup again. "I have no idea who you're talking about."

He leaned back. "You will tell me."

Jayda froze, teacup halfway to her lips. Her pulse beat hot in her ears. She forced herself to sip, forced herself to breathe, forced herself to smile when Ginny teased Ed about his terrible memory for dates.

But the only voice she heard was Michael's threat.

If he pressed, if he dragged the truth out of her here at this table, everything would collapse. The fragile façade she was building—the grateful foster daughter, the success story, the soon-to-be lawyer—would shatter, leaving only...the girl from the streets.

She met Michael's eyes with a practiced coolness. "Enjoy the wait," she whispered back, and turned to laugh at something Uncle Henry said.

Before Michael could respond, a new voice carried across the car. "Well, well, if it isn't Jayda Simone."

She looked up—and her breath caught. The door slid closed with Simon Blair standing in front of it.

He approached the end of the table, tall and broad-shouldered, his smile as easy as she remembered. Time had carved a stronger jawline, a deeper confidence in his stance, but the same charm gleamed in his eyes. He spread his arms wide as though to encompass the entire train in his delight. "I haven't seen you in years. Come here, you."

Jayda rose automatically, and Simon pulled her into a warm, enveloping hug. He smelled of a sharp cologne and crisp winter air. He must have been outside for fresh air. She could use some too. For a moment, she allowed herself to lean into Simon's old familiarity, his quick acceptance. He had been a friendly face during her time at the Blairs'...and a handsome one to admire from afar.

"Look at you," Simon said as he stepped back, still holding her shoulders. "A lawyer. I'd hate to go toe to toe with you in court. You'd chew me up and spit me out."

"Oh, stop," she said, managing a laugh. "Like you could do anything wrong that would even get you there."

He threw his head back and laughed, smooth as ever, as though flirtation were his second language. His gaze swept her face, and Jayda felt a flush rise unbidden. She knew he was a player. His attention meant nothing. But she enjoyed the interest however fake.

"Man, you are stunning," Simon said, glancing over at Michael. "Your sister turned out to be a real beauty."

Jayda jolted at Simon's word choice. A glance at Michael's daggers in his eyes showed he didn't like being called her sibling.

The feeling was mutual.

"No relation," she said to Simon. "Not even friends, right, Michael?"

Ginny cut in, scolding, "Jayda, be nice. You too, Michael. You two always fought like a couple of chihuahuas with one bone."

The twins laughed with glee, and Ginny tickled Tyler's belly.

"My apologies, Aunt Ginny," Simon said, hand on chest,

admonished at causing a stir so soon into the trip. "We'll behave. Promise. Jayda, let me escort you to your cabin," Simon said gallantly, offering his arm. "I'm sure you'd like to settle your things and maybe take a breather, yes?"

The man was also a mind reader.

Before Jayda could answer, two small voices shrieked behind her. "Jayda! Jayda!"

The Blairs' foster twins, bundles of mischief and curls, jumped out of their seats and hurled themselves against her legs. She staggered, laughing despite herself, as little arms wrapped tight around her.

"What's your names?" she asked, wrapping her arms around each of their shoulders. They were two little boys who needed to know they weren't mistakes in this world—a feeling she struggled with her entire life. Always wondering if her mother would have died if she hadn't needed to provide for her. And after her mother's death, Jayda only had more doubts about her reason on this earth. A career in family law would finally give her a place and a cause.

One that helped children like these boys.

"I'm Timmy!" the one with the red shirt announced.

"Nice to meet you, Timmy. And that means you must be Tommy," Jayda said, suppressing a smile.

"No! I'm not Tommy. I'm Tyler."

Jayda smiled at Simon. "Oh, my mistake. Tyler, how could I forget? Well, it's nice to meet you both."

"You're so pretty!" Timmy exclaimed, looking up with wide adoring eyes.

The other nodded emphatically. "Can we go with you? We don't want to sit with boring grown-ups."

Simon chuckled. "See? Even the kids agree with me. But boys, I asked first."

Jayda bent to hug the twins, her heart tugging in directions she didn't expect. Their tiny hands, their fierce affection

—it reminded her of herself at their age. Of clinging to her mother before the hospital machines and chemotherapy stole her away. Of clinging to foster siblings who came and went, their faces fading like shadows.

She brushed a hand over one twin's hair. "I'd love for you to walk with me."

"Can I sleep in your cabin?" Timmy, the more daring of the two, piped up.

Jayda's eyes flicked instinctively to Michael. He sat back in his chair, brows raised, watching the scene like a silent judge.

Her throat tightened. She turned back to Timmy and forced a grin. "Sure," she said softly. "That would be fun. If it's okay with Ginny."

The twins cheered and wrapped her in another crushing hug. But when she looked up at Simon, his stiff expression caused her concern. Had he been serious about alone time with her? She had thought he was joking. Timmy and Tyler were children. How silly and immature of the man to be upset about the boys joining them.

Jayda stood. "I really don't need an escort to my cabin."

Simon flashed a smile, all irritation gone. Perhaps she had been wrong? "I wouldn't miss it. Shall we, everyone?"

Aunt Caroline handed Simon his keycards, and he scooped up Timmy and put him on his hip. The image felt off, this classily dressed man with a child in his arms.

But somehow it worked, and now Jayda saw a different side of the handsome man.

Perhaps Simon Blair was father material.

Not that Jayda was looking to get married and have children. Her career would always come first. She had no time to entertain the possibility of a relationship—or of being a wife and mother.

"If you insist," she said, reaching for her backpack on the back of her chair.

"After you." Simon gestured.

They made it to the sliding door before she realized Michael had taken Tyler into his arms and was following them.

~

Michael trailed them, the picture of casual disinterest—or so he told himself—but his eyes had locked on Simon's hand which had lingered too long on Jayda's arm back in the dining car. Simon always had that kind of charm, the kind that slid off his tongue like honey and fooled half the girls he met. Smooth, polished, effortless. A politician in the making, if he ever wanted to run for office.

And now he was using it on Jayda.

Michael's jaw tightened. He didn't know why it bothered him. Jayda Simone was nothing but trouble—had been since she was fourteen and strutted into his house with that mix of defiance and mischief. She had a way of stirring things up without even trying. She'd grown up to be the same type of woman—dangerous.

Simon leaned closer as they walked down the narrow corridor of the train, whispering something that made Jayda's lips curve. Not quite a laugh but close enough to heat Michael's blood.

"Jayda! Wait for us!" Tyler shouted from Michael's arms.

Jayda looked back, but her gaze met Michael's, silently asking why he was with them. He wanted to tell her he was there for her protection, but that she would never receive well. She needed it, regardless of what she believed. She was dangerous, but Simon was trouble.

When Jayda stopped at room 18, he realized she was next to his 19. He hadn't been expecting his mother to put them so close. He held his tongue about announcing the find.

"Will you look at that?" Simon said. "We're neighbors. Room 17. If I get scared, maybe I'll knock."

Michael snorted. The man had nerve. Michael opened his mouth to intervene, but Jayda glanced back at him, almost as if she was daring him to say anything. But why? He wasn't her keeper. He wasn't anything to her. But he didn't like the way Simon hovered so close to her, eyes glinting with a cocky smile.

"Sure," Jayda said lightly, giving Timothy's cheek a playful squeeze then taking him from Simon. "We'll help you if you get scared, won't we, Timmy and Tyler?"

Simon chuckled, leaning against the wall like he owned the train. "Not really what I had in mind."

That did it. Michael stepped forward, sliding in beside Jayda and putting Tyler down beside his brother. Michael's shoulder brushed Jayda's. "Take the hint, Simon. That was a don't bother knocking."

Jayda's eyes narrowed. "Excuse me? You don't speak for me, Michael."

Michael stammered, realizing what he had just done, as if it was any of his business. "I just mean you don't know who else is on this train, and...and if you're opening your door to anyone who knocks, it could be dangerous." His voice was sharper than he had intended, but he wasn't backing down. Not with Simon watching, smirk widening. The con man was setting his sights on *Jayda* of all people.

Not that Michael should care at all, which he didn't. But he'd seen enough crime in his job to recognize a disaster brewing.

Simon lifted an eyebrow. "I think Jayda can take care of herself, Mike. The woman's an attorney."

"Well, technically not yet," Jayda said.

Simon continued as though she hadn't spoken. "Or is it me you have an issue with, cuz?"

Michael glared at Simon. "I have an issue with people being taken advantage of."

"Oh, please, Michael," Jayda interrupted. "You act like you're some crusader. You would have kicked me to the curb if Ginny had let you."

"Yes, because you took advantage of my parents."

As soon as the words were out of his mouth, Michael wished to suck them back in. The shock on Jayda's face dulled to misty eyes.

"I think I need to...go lie down. Excuse me." Jayda fumbled to open her door.

Michael touched her shoulder. "I'm sorry. That came out wrong."

"Way to go, cousin," Simon said. "And you accuse me of brewing up a disaster. I'd say you've got that covered all on your own."

"Can we stay with you? Please, please, pleeease?" Timmy whined, his wide eyes flashing up at Jayda, begging.

Jayda bent low, laughing softly, brushing a strand of hair from her face. "I don't think the conductor would approve of an all-night slumber party."

"But you said we could," Timmy insisted, a pout forming.

Michael caught the flicker of hesitation in Jayda's eyes. She was cornered.

And *he* had caused her to be. Not Simon but him.

Simon chuckled with an ease Michael detested...and envied. "Come on, you two. How about some ice cream?" He bent down, his voice lowering to a teasing whisper. "Though I can't say I blame you for wanting to hang out with Jayda."

"Yay!" Tyler shouted and jumped into Simon's arms.

The hall closed in on Michael, stealing his breath from his lungs. His plan to help Jayda had only made him the bad guy.

Timmy pulled Jayda's hand. "Come with us for ice cream."

Jayda pushed open the door to two bunks, a narrow fold-down seat, barely enough room for four people to stand without bumping shoulders.

"As yummy as that sounds, I think I'm going to rest for a little while. Simon, would you take the boys for their treat?"

"Absolutely," Simon said. He ushered Jayda into her cabin, his hand grazing her back, and Michael fought the impulse to grab his cousin by the collar.

Jayda glanced around, smile brittle at the edges. "Cozy."

"Claustrophobic," Michael muttered.

"Homey," Simon countered, throwing him a grin that was equal parts challenge and charm.

Michael snorted before he could stop himself.

Jayda turned his way, those sharp dark eyes narrowing on him. "What's your problem?"

"My problem," Michael said, crossing his arms, "is that I don't buy this little act you're putting on. You don't fool me, Jayda. Something's going on. I want to know who those men were. Tell me, and I'll leave you alone."

The twins went silent, sensing the shift. Even Simon's smile dimmed, and his eyes narrowed at Michael.

Jayda's mask snapped back into place. "It's none of your business."

"Correction," Michael said, voice low. "It is my business. Because whatever mess you're tangled in, you dragged it to this train. With my family."

"I would never put your family at risk."

"For your sake, I hope not."

Simon whistled softly, amused. "Well, aren't you two entertaining? What's this danger you're talking about?"

"Nothing," both Michael and Jayda said simultaneously, daring each other to say more.

Simon's eyebrows arched in disbelief. "You'll have to do

better than that. But fine, play that game. Let's go, boys. Ice cream awaits. These two have something going on."

Jayda scoffed, heat rushing to her cheeks. "Not even close."

Michael wanted to agree. He should have agreed. Instead, he glared at Simon, silently daring him to keep pushing.

The twins, oblivious to the deeper tension, tugged on Jayda's sleeve. "Can we please sleep here tonight?"

Jayda softened immediately, touching their hair tenderly. "Do you promise to behave?"

Michael leaned back, arms crossed, watching the scene with a complicated twist in his chest. She looked...natural with them. The instant connection between them surprised him. Her kindness toward them caught him off guard. It wasn't like her to care. But it was obvious that she did.

And for some reason, that thought unsettled him more than Simon's flirting.

What else had he missed about Jayda? And was it too late to change that?

The memory of those men with guns said it couldn't be, no matter how much she pushed him away.

"I'll be next door if you need me," Michael said, exiting the cabin.

"Don't worry, she won't." Simon smirked. He handed his extra key card to Jayda. "Just in case," he said to her with a wink, and the two left Michael behind.

Michael stood in the narrow hallway. The air in the tight space grew thick with unspoken tension. Three adults in a space too small for their egos, their secrets, their suspicions.

And it was only day one.

Four

The steady clatter of the train against the rails should have been soothing. A lullaby of iron wheels carrying her further away from New Haven, away from the library, away from the man's furious face the moment she'd pulled the trigger on the stun gun. Instead, the train's rhythm scraped against Jayda's raw nerves, a relentless reminder that she was running and not safe.

She shifted in her narrow bunk, pressing the side of her face into the pillow that smelled faintly of starch. Beside her, on the opposite bunk, the twins breathed in sync. Little saws, soft snores—the sound of safety, of innocence. They had the kind of sleep only children could manage.

Jayda envied them.

Every time she closed her eyes, the day's events moved in her memory. The heavy boots slammed against the pavement when the men chased her. The angry hiss of breath when they tried to reach for her but she'd escaped their grasp. She half-expected them to burst into the cabin now, snatch her up, and drag her into the snowy night.

Who were they? The mob? They had to be. The man

wanted the file of the woman who turned state's evidence and disappeared right after. Was the man she tasered the released convict that Professor D mentioned? If so, she was a dead woman.

Jayda hugged her knees, tucking herself small in the bunk, a makeshift hiding place on a holiday train bound for California. Snow stacked against the windows as the train barreled into a storm in the dark.

Would she ever go back?

The question curled sharply in her chest. If this man had her name, would she even live long enough to walk across a stage at graduation?

Which wasn't even an option anymore anyway.

She pressed the heel of her palm against her eyes. The rumble of the train deepened as it pushed into a wall of wind. Snow streaked the window in ribbons, catching her attention. She sat up, pulling the blanket around her shoulders, and leaned toward the glass. The outside world vanished with just a blur of white swallowing the view.

"Great," she whispered. "Outrun the mob but die in a snowdrift."

Her breath clouded faintly against the window. She traced a circle with her finger, her mind spinning back—not to the faceless men she feared but to two others.

Michael and Simon.

Her mouth tightened.

Michael, with his half-smirk, his reporter's curiosity that always saw more than she wanted him to, and Simon with his slick smile, expensive watch, and a suave charm that always set her guard on high alert. They'd both sidled up to her too quickly, offered help too easily. Men like that tended to have a price tag tucked behind their words.

They both wanted something from her.

She couldn't tell what yet.

But she knew this much: they weren't getting it.

She had enough on her plate—classwork, survival, trying not to crumble under the weight of fear every time she heard footsteps in the corridor. She didn't have time for them, or their interests, or whatever schemes they hid behind polite smiles.

She would tell them both to leave her alone. Tomorrow.

A soft knock startled her. She froze, blanket clutched to her chest, heart slamming.

Michael's warning from earlier surfaced like a lighthouse beam in her memory. It's dangerous to open the door to strangers.

She swallowed hard, leaned close. "Who is it?" she whispered.

The reply was quiet, feminine. "Jayda? It's Ginny. How are the boys? They being good for you?"

Relief sagged Jayda's shoulders, though the tension didn't fully leave. She glanced at the bunk—two tousle-haired heads, still lost in sleep.

"They're fine," she said through the door, careful to keep her voice low.

There was a pause. Then Ginny's voice, softer still. "Will you open the door? I just want to see for myself. And..." A beat of hesitation. "I want to know you're all right."

Jayda closed her eyes. Ginny meant well—she always had. She'd been the closest thing Jayda had had to a mother during those years in foster care. But that was the problem, wasn't it? Ginny always wanted to step into shoes that didn't fit. No one could fill the void her actual mother had left.

Her throat tightened. "Maybe in the morning," she said, forcing gentleness. "It's late. Let's...talk then."

A pause. Then a small, sad, "Okay."

The footsteps receded. Jayda exhaled, leaning back against the pillow.

She barely had time to settle before another knock rattled the door.

Her sigh came sharp, frustrated. Ginny again?

She pushed to her feet, shoving her arms into the sleeves of her sweatshirt. Her foster mom would never understand that this conversation couldn't be forced. Jayda didn't want her to play mother now, not after all these years.

But fine. Tonight, she'd let Ginny fuss and get it out of her system.

Jayda pulled the sweatshirt over her head, padded barefoot across the cabin floor, and tugged open the lock.

Her blood iced.

Not Ginny.

A man.

Dark jacket, sharp shoulders, eyes like black glass fixed on her, but his face was in the shadows of the dark corridor.

Jayda reacted on instinct—shoving the door, trying to slam it shut. His hand caught the edge, pushing back. The wood bit into her palms as she leaned her weight against it, desperate.

The twins woke with sharp cries, the high, frightened sound of children jarred awake.

"Jayda!" one of them screamed.

The man's face was too close. His breath slid through the crack. She shoved harder, fear surging hot in her veins.

Then a violent bang. The door snapped inward, slammed shut, and he was gone.

The twins sobbed in their bunks, little fists clutching blankets. Jayda's hands shook on the lock, her pulse pounding so loud it drowned the storm outside.

Another knock—this one harder, insistent.

"Jayda, open up!" Michael's voice.

"Now!" Simon chimed in, urgent and sharp.

Her fingers fumbled with the lock. She yanked the door

open to have Michael burst into the cabin just as the train screamed on its brakes. The grinding halt pitched Jayda sideways, and she flew straight into Michael's arms.

~

Jayda trembled in his arms, her body soft against his, fragile even, and yet there was a current of defiance running through her that practically vibrated in his chest. She still held him back from knowing the truth.

Since spotting those men at the platform, he had this gut-deep certainty that Jayda wasn't safe. And now, that idea had just materialized into reality. He'd been right. She was in trouble. And now, having her in his arms, the last thing he wanted was to release her.

But she stiffened, pushing at his chest. "Let me go, Michael," she demanded, her voice low, sharp, as though she was trying to wrestle control back from whatever had just happened.

He hesitated. For a second too long.

"Jayda—"

"Now."

The steel in her eyes made his hands unclasp reluctantly. He forced himself to step away as far as the cabin would allow.

Simon, ever the helpful boy scout, crouched near the twins, whispering something soothing that made the boys' sobs taper down into little hiccups. Michael's jaw clenched. He should be the one steadying the kids, not Simon playing hero.

Jayda adjusted her sweatshirt, her gaze flitting away from Michael's. "It was just...someone who had the wrong room. That's all."

Michael's brows drew together. "You didn't know him?"

"No." Her answer was swift, clipped. "I've never seen him before."

But she wasn't looking at him when she said it.

Michael studied her, seeing more in what she didn't say than what she did. She was being careful with her words. This wasn't one of the men who'd chased her to the train—whoever they were. This was someone else. A new threat. Which meant things were escalating.

"What about—"

"I said I've never seen him. I meant what I said."

She wanted him to drop it. But how could he?

"Were you hurt?"

Jayda folded her arms. "No. Don't worry about me. I don't need your help. I'm fine."

His teeth ground together. That wasn't true. She was still shaking.

"At least give me a description," he pressed, sliding into reporter mode because that was the only way he knew to disarm her defenses. "Height? Build? What was he wearing?"

She huffed out an impatient sigh. "It was dark. A hat, maybe? I don't know. It's nothing to worry about."

"He tried to get in here. That's not nothing."

"Michael." She cut him off, her tone sharp as a snapped icicle. "Let it go. Find out why the train stopped instead of interrogating me."

As if on cue, a knock rattled the cabin door, followed by the sound of the conductor's voice urging everyone to calm down. The corridor buzzed with mutters and worried questions. Michael opened the door, and the conductor explained, "The train hit something. An animal, most likely. With the snowstorm, we had to stop and check the tracks. We'll be moving again shortly. Everyone, please return to your cabins."

Michael nodded but didn't release the man immediately.

"Be on the lookout. A man in a hat tried to barge into this cabin. Not drunk—deliberate."

The conductor's expression flickered uneasily. "We'll keep an eye out."

Jayda crossed her arms tighter, her glare practically scorching at Michael. "You're exaggerating. He was probably under the influence and got confused about his room."

She turned away from him to face Simon. "Thank you for helping with the boys. You were wonderful." Her smile for Simon was soft, grateful, the smile Michael had never seen her aim at him. "You're so kind, Simon. You'll make a good father someday."

Simon flushed, ducking his head modestly, eating it up.

Michael wanted to punch the wall.

"Could you help me bring the twins to Ginny?" Jayda asked, placing her trust squarely in Simon as if Michael wasn't standing two feet away.

"Of course." Simon gently herded the boys toward the door.

And just like that, Jayda, Simon, and the twins disappeared down the corridor, leaving Michael alone in her cabin, seething.

He raked a frustrated hand through his hair. How could she dismiss what just happened? How could she not see this wasn't some random lost or drunk person but something calculated?

She had to know. She wasn't being honest for a reason.

And Simon, playing the part of the noble protector, soaked up Jayda's thanks while Michael stood painted as the nuisance. Simon was up to something too. The guy hovered too close, too eager. Michael meant to find out what was going on with both of them.

As he turned to leave the cabin, something on the floor in

the corridor caught his eye. A folded piece of paper, almost camouflaged against the shadows on the floor.

He bent down and picked it up. The edges were creased from being handled. Curious, he unfolded it.

A list of names stared back at him, twenty in total, scrawled in a neat but hurried hand. Each name carried a checkmark beside it—except for the last two.

Veronica Carlisle and Jayda Simone.

Jayda's name was written there, stark and undeniable. Unchecked.

His stomach dropped.

The air seemed to thin around him as his journalist instincts flared into overdrive. Michael sat down on the edge of the bunk and pulled out his phone, quickly typing the first name into a search bar.

An obituary popped up instantly. Dead. Car crash.

Second name—another obituary. Fire.

Third—accidental drowning.

His pulse pounded harder with each search. Every single person on the list was dead. Strange accidents. Convenient accidents.

It didn't take long before the conclusion crystallized in his mind, cold and certain.

This was a hit list.

A hollow dread pooled in Michael's chest. Whoever had barged into Jayda's cabin wasn't drunk. He wasn't lost. He was a hitman.

And Jayda was on his list.

Five

The dining car smelled like bacon, coffee, and cinnamon rolls—comforting scents that should have wrapped the morning in coziness, except Jayda's nerves were still frayed from the night before. She slid into her seat at the long table Ginny had claimed for the entire family, grateful for the steaming mug of coffee already waiting for her.

Ginny was in full hostess mode, her curls bouncing as she made sure everyone had plates. "Eat up, everyone," she sang out. "Big day ahead! We'll be rolling into Chicago tonight, and I have fantastic plans."

Jayda forced a smile, though she wasn't sure she could stomach much. Sleep had come in fits and starts, taunted by the memory of the man in her cabin, his hands grasping, his breathing a hiss in her ear before Michael had appeared and scared him off. The liquid in her mug jostled from her trembling hand, and she put it down. She couldn't let her fear show.

The twins were chattering at a speed only they could understand, piling scrambled eggs onto their plates like they were in some kind of eating competition. Uncle Henry sat beside them, already resigned to cleaning up spilled juice. Across from Jayda, Aunt Caroline adjusted her scarf and cleared her throat.

"Simon will be down later," she said with a prim smile. "You know he's always been a late riser."

Michael, sitting too close to Jayda on her left, gave a low scoff into his coffee.

Jayda's head snapped toward him, eyes narrowing. "Knock it off," she muttered under her breath.

Michael arched a brow at her, feigning innocence.

She raised her voice enough for everyone at the table to hear. "Simon was wonderful with the boys last night. When they were scared, he calmed them down, made them laugh. He deserves a little extra sleep."

Caroline gave Jayda a grateful smile, though Michael's eyes rolled so hard she thought they might stick in the back of his head.

Jayda ignored him and stabbed at her eggs, pretending her pulse wasn't racing from the tension between them. Why did he care so much about what she said about Simon anyway?

Conversation rolled on about Chicago—shopping, sightseeing, and the layover they would have there. Jayda tried to focus on her plate, but then she felt Michael lean in, his voice pitched low just for her.

"Who is Veronica Carlisle?"

Her fork froze midair. "Excuse me?"

"You heard me," he said, his eyes fixed straight ahead, not even looking at her. His hand brushed under the table, sliding something small and folded into her lap.

Her fingers curled around it instinctively, hiding the paper in her palm.

"What is this?" she whispered.

"Something your visitor left behind last night," Michael murmured. His jaw was tight, his expression calm for the family's sake. "It's a list. You're on it. You and Veronica are the only two still breathing." He finally glanced at her, his gaze sharp. "For now."

Before Jayda could respond, Ginny clapped her hands. "All right, everyone! Tonight, during our stop in Chicago, we're going to the Santa's Village Christmas Dinner! They're setting up an entire North Pole experience in the hotel ballroom. Santa, reindeer, the works. And every single one of you must attend. I've also booked a room for everyone to relax and freshen up."

The twins erupted into cheers, shouting, "Santa!" They bounced in their seats.

Caroline reached for her tea, saying, "Simon will be there, of course. He wouldn't miss it."

Jayda forced another smile, but her grip tightened on the folded paper in her lap.

Ginny beamed at the boys. "Christmas is only a week and a half away, and I want us to savor every moment together. Which brings me to my next surprise." She reached into her bag and pulled out a stack of wrapped boxes, small and square, decorated in festive paper. "Every morning, I'll give each of you a gift. But you mustn't be late for breakfast—this is when I'll hand out the holiday orders for the day's festivities."

The twins nearly fell out of their chairs with excitement, clawing at their boxes.

Jayda mustered a laugh, even as dread curled low in her stomach.

"I need to study, Ginny," she reminded gently. "My tests don't go away just because it's Christmas."

"Then Michael will help you," Ginny declared without hesitation. "That's settled."

Michael looked smug. "Happy to."

Jayda opened her mouth to protest, but before she could, a smooth voice slipped in behind her.

"I'll help her."

Simon.

Jayda stiffened as his hands came down lightly on her shoulders, warm and casual, like he belonged there. He leaned down just close enough that his breath brushed her ear. "Wouldn't want you falling behind, Jayda."

Her heart thudded. She glanced sideways just in time to catch Michael's glare, hot and unmistakable. He wasn't even trying to hide it. Then his gaze dropped—to the note still clenched in her hand beneath the table.

Jayda's throat tightened. She crumpled the paper in her fist, shoving it into her pocket for later.

"I don't need anyone's help," she said sharply, pushing back from the table. Chairs scraped as she stood. "Excuse me. I'm...I'm tired after last night."

Ginny frowned, but Jayda didn't wait for permission. She turned and hurried out of the dining car, feeling Simon and Michael's eyes burning between her shoulder blades.

When she finally reached the quiet of her cabin, she shut the door, leaned back against it, and let out a shaky breath.

Only then did she pull the paper from her pocket and smooth it open.

A list.

Names scrawled in hurried ink. Most crossed out. The two at the bottom were not.

Veronica Carlisle.

Jayda Simone.

Her fingers trembled as she reached for her bag. She dug through books and papers until she pulled out the old photograph and case file she'd hidden since that night in the law library. The file that man had tried to steal.

She flipped it open. The first name on the report glared at her, stark and undeniable.

Veronica Carlisle.

The same name written above her own on the list.

In the library, Jayda hadn't just interrupted a man stealing a file. She'd interrupted a hit job.

And now, she was on the list.

Jayda stood and grabbed her bag, heading for the door.

Michael stalked down the narrow corridor of the sleeper car, his breath uneven. He'd checked Jayda's cabin twice. Empty. Knocked on his parents' and Caroline and Henry's. No sign.

Where was she?

He moved quickly, each step vibrating faintly with the rhythm of the train as it cut through the wintry Midwest. His gut twisted. Something was wrong. He knew it with the same certainty that he knew how many words he could squeeze into an article lede before an editor red-lined it. Jayda was not the type to disappear quietly.

Michael pushed through the swaying door into the next car. He leaned against the frame for balance and scanned the seating section. Businessmen with laptops. A pair of teenage girls sharing earbuds. A woman rocking a toddler with flushed cheeks. No Jayda.

He checked the bathrooms one by one, ignoring the odd looks when he rattled a locked door and muttered, "Sorry."

She was not on the train. But how was that possible?

His pulse hammered harder. Every second he didn't find her was another second she could be checked off that list.

The dining car was next. He shoved open the door and stepped inside, his eyes sweeping across the room. A few passengers lingered over late coffee, the tang of syrup and toast still hanging in the air.

Michael walked the length of the car, scanning each booth. His voice came out rough, more desperate than he had intended. “Have any of you seen a woman? Black curls. Dark eyes. She’s...” His throat caught, but he forced the words out. “She’s really pretty.”

He froze at his own admission.

Really pretty.

He hadn’t planned to say that. He’d meant to say short, or maybe young, or possibly stubborn. But the truth had slipped out before he could catch it, and it startled him enough that he actually faltered mid-stride. Because it was true. Jayda had always been beautiful. Not in the polished, curated way of New York socialites he sometimes brushed shoulders with at events, but in a way that felt natural and comforting.

And now, seeing her as an adult...her beauty was sharper. More stunning—smart. And somehow, she tugged at places in his chest he’d worked hard to keep barricaded.

But there was no time to think about that. She was missing with a killer on the train. And she was on his list.

A woman at one table tilted her head. “I think I saw someone who fits that description. She went into Room 19. Back in the cabins.”

Michael’s breath caught.

Room 19.

His room.

He hadn’t checked there. Because why would Jayda—?

He didn’t wait to finish the thought. He bolted.

The corridor felt narrower on the sprint back. He fumbled for his key card even before he reached the door, his hand slick with sweat despite the drafty chill of the train.

He shoved the key in, the lock beeped, and he threw the door open.

And stopped dead.

Jayda sat on the bench across from his unmade bunk, her curls framing her face like a storm cloud. She was holding a folded sheet of paper in her lap. Her posture was unnervingly still, except for her eyes—wide and carrying both defiance and fear.

Michael stepped in and shut the door behind him. The lock clicked, a small sound swallowed by the rumble of the tracks.

Jayda didn't flinch. Didn't look up right away. Then, with a voice flat but edged with fragility, she said, "I need your help."

Michael froze at her words.

Jayda never asked anyone for help, not when they were kids, not when she was dropped into his mother's house with nothing but a plastic grocery bag of clothes, not when she grew up and clawed her way through school. She was stubborn and relentless, but most of all, independent. And now she was sitting on his bench seat, framed by the dim train light, clutching papers like they might vanish in her hands, and asking him for help.

"What are those?" he asked, his voice sharper than intended.

Her eyes flicked up, dark and worried, before returning to the sheets of paper.

"It's why they're after me," she whispered. "These papers are from a law file. This all started in the Yale library. A man was stealing it. I tried to stop him. He attacked me and dropped it."

Michael sat in a slump on his bed across from her. "He attacked you?"

She nodded with a wave of her hand. "I tasered him and got away. But I grabbed these papers on my way out."

Michael's stomach dropped. He leaned closer, feeling the sway of the train under him. "You *tasered* him?"

She lifted her chin at him. "He had a gun. I did what I had to do. It doesn't matter, Michael. What matters is this name." She tapped the page with her finger. "Veronica Carlisle. She was listed as a witness. These documents show she testified and then disappeared. Possibly witness protection. These are pictures of her."

Michael frowned, trying to chase the connection. He reached out, and after a hesitation, she handed him the pages. His journalist's eye devoured them quickly—typed notes, a government seal, but on the top, Veronica's name was listed as a witness...the same name on the hit-list.

"She's next," Michael muttered.

"Yes, and so am I," Jayda finished. Her voice cracked just enough to betray the fear she held back. "But what if they need this file to figure out where she really went? Whoever wants her gone...they won't stop until they have these."

Michael stared at the name. His throat went dry. Veronica Carlisle. He'd never heard of her before, but he'd seen this sort of document before—in exposés about witness tampering, organized crime hits, leaks inside protective custody. A cold weight settled in his chest.

"And these pictures," Jayda said, tugging another sheet from the folded mess in her lap. She held it up. A grainy black-and-white photo, clearly an old surveillance image of a woman stepping off the platform of a train, her hair pulled tight and her head low. "These were in the file too. They're looking for her."

Michael caught himself rubbing the back of his neck, a nervous tic he hated. "And you're sure this isn't just some old, irrelevant—"

"No." Her eyes locked on his, fierce and cutting. "I've been chased. Cornered. I almost didn't make it to this train alive. Somebody wants these documents. And I can't do this alone, Michael. I need—"

She stopped short, swallowed.

Michael let out a breath, dropped the paper onto the bunk. "You're asking me for my *journalistic help,* then?"

"Yes." Her tone was clipped, defensive. "You know how to dig. How to follow trails. If anyone can figure out who Veronica Carlisle really was and where she went, it's you."

For a long moment, heavy silence wrapped around them. Michael leaned against the wall, folding his arms, studying her. Jayda, always too composed, always refusing to let him or anyone see the cracks, now stared at him like he was her last lifeline.

But he couldn't let it be that simple.

"Do you really want my help?" he asked quietly.

Her brow furrowed. "I just said—"

"No." He cut her off, his voice lower now, steadier. "Do you really want it? Because if you do...I want something, too."

Her mouth parted, then snapped shut. Her eyes narrowed in suspicion. "Of course. There it is. The catch."

"Jayda—"

She stood, folding the papers with quick, jerky hands, shoving them against her chest. Her curls bounced as she shook her head. "Forget it. I should've known. You've always wanted me gone. Out of your perfect family. Out of your mother's house. Out of your life."

"That's not—"

"You'll have to talk to Ginny about that," she snapped. "She's the one who kept me, who insisted I stay, who made me family whether you—or I—liked it. If you want me out, talk to her."

She turned, heading for the door, but Michael's hand shot out before he could stop himself. His fingers wrapped around hers, warm and trembling.

"Wait," he said.

She froze, half-turned, her breath quick. He tugged her gently back, not enough to hurt, but enough to make her face him.

Their eyes collided. The train swayed. Time stretched between them.

"My mother loves you," he said roughly. "You know that, right?"

Jayda blinked, startled.

"And Dad too. You are...you *are* family. To them. That's all I'm asking for. That you recognize how much they love you." His voice softened, betraying more than he intended. "And I—" He stopped, jaw tightening. He wasn't ready to peel back that last layer, not with her life on the line.

Her lips parted, caught between disbelief and skepticism. "You what?"

Michael's hand was still around hers. He could feel the pulse in her wrist, rapid against his fingers.

He should let go. He didn't.

Michael swallowed hard, refusing to let the words that had almost escaped his mouth have air. She was important—far too important—but he'd never let himself admit that, not even in the privacy of his own mind. Instead, he forced the tightening in his chest down and reached for safer ground.

"Never mind." He cleared his throat. "How did you even get in here without a key?" His voice was rougher than he meant, but he let his words anchor him to reason. Keep this meeting business.

Jayda's lips tilted, not in a smile but in the barest acknowledgment of what she'd done. She shrugged. "I lifted it from your wallet."

His brows rose. "You—what?" He reached for his wallet, finding his second key gone.

"A little trick I learned when I was young. You really shouldn't leave your wallet on the table like that. You're asking for trouble."

Michael let out a disbelieving huff, trying to mask the

worry clawing at his ribs. "I should've guessed. Learned it on the streets, I suppose?"

Her head snapped up, curls framing her face in defiance. "No. I learned it at a foster home. Before Ginny and Ed." Her gaze didn't waver, but her voice lowered, quieter. "When my foster father locked me in a closet. I figured out where he kept the key."

The words hit him like a physical blow. Michael's breath caught, and for a second, he couldn't think, couldn't move. All he saw was a younger Jayda—too small and scared, hidden behind a door.

"Jayda..." His throat tightened. "I'm—" His voice faltered, then steadied with raw sincerity. "I'm so sorry."

Her eyes softened just a fraction, though she gave a small shake of her head, as though to dismiss his pity before it weakened her. She gripped the papers tighter, holding them like a shield. "Will you help me or not?"

Michael straightened, resolve pulling him forward. "Yes. Whatever you need."

Her shoulders lowered, relief flickering across her face for the first time since he had found her here. "Then I need to know where the real Veronica Carlisle went."

Before he could respond, the train jolted, brakes whining against metal as the conductor's voice filled the overhead speakers. *"Next stop, Chicago Union Station. Please gather your belongings..."*

Michael leaned back, dragging in a deep breath. Perfect timing. They had work to do during the layover.

He glanced at Jayda, who still clutched the papers close.

"Looks like we'll be late," he said.

Her brows knit. "Late for what?"

"The Santa Village dinner." His mouth curved faintly, but the weight in his voice kept it from being light. "I'll let you be the one to break it to Mom."

Jayda blinked, then a laugh escaped her, soft and unguarded. "Sure. Make me the bad guy."

Michael didn't laugh with her. He watched her instead, his chest tightening. Slowly, he stood and drew her close to him. "There are enough bad guys already." His tone was low, steady, but charged with warning. He lowered his voice as the train slowed further. "Stay close to me, Jayda."

Her laughter faded. She nodded once, the bravado slipping away.

"I'm trusting you," she whispered. "Don't make me regret it."

Michael realized that, for Jayda to come to him took more strength in her than if she tried to do this alone. He was sure he was the last person in the world she would ever trust. And she wasn't wrong. He didn't deserve her trust.

But duty called.

He could practically hear his mother telling him to help Jayda. But what if protecting her was more than duty? What if he'd been waiting for her to trust him all along?

If so, then he had one shot. He doubted Jayda gave second chances to anyone.

Six

Ginny shouted with glee. "I knew it," she said, grinning like Christmas morning had arrived early. "The two of you—finally sitting down and talking things through. Do you know how long I've prayed for this? Our family needed healing, and here it is, right in front of me. It's a Christmas miracle."

Jayda kept her arms folded tight across her chest, more for armor than warmth, as Michael's mother prattled on. Ginny's face glowed with earnest excitement, her hands fluttering as she spoke.

Jayda forced a smile. A miracle? More like a nightmare she couldn't wake from. If only Ginny knew that the only reason she and Michael stood together was because men with guns were hunting her down for whatever was buried in the documents she had stuffed in her bag.

Michael cleared his throat. "Mom, we've got a few things to sort out. Personal matters. It might take a little time."

"Oh, don't worry about dinner," Ginny said, her eyes twinkling. "I'll hold off until you're back. Just don't be too late. We're all taking a family photo with Santa at the village, and you can't miss it. Then the train leaves at nine sharp—through the Rockies! A winter wonderland."

Jayda managed another smile, though the task they had weighed down on her. Three hours. That was all they had. Three hours to untangle the mystery of Veronica Carlisle before the train pulled out of the station.

Ginny hugged them both, whispering, "I'm so glad this reunion is happening."

"Me too," Jayda mumbled. If only Ginny knew the truth.

They slipped out of the station and onto the bustling street, holiday lights casting a festive glow over everything. Jayda tried to steady her breathing. Every step away from the family meant freedom—until a familiar voice called out.

"Wait up."

Jayda stiffened. Simon. Michael's cousin moved quickly through the crowd, his scarf trailing over his coat. He looked annoyed that they had left him behind.

"What's really going on?" Simon asked, falling into step beside them. His sharp gaze flicked between Jayda and Michael. "You expect me to believe you two are suddenly patching up twelve years of vitriol over a slice of pie? Come on."

Jayda exhaled slowly. "Simon, it would be safer if you didn't know."

"Safer? Safe from that man last night?" His eyes narrowed. "What about Michael's safety? You're dragging him into something, aren't you?"

Jayda flinched at the truth in his words. She *was* dragging Michael deeper into danger. For a second, she wondered if she should do this alone. That way, only her neck was on the line.

But Michael's jaw tightened as he spoke. "I've handled dangerous investigations before. I know what I'm doing."

"So what? I can hold my own too. Don't act like I'm fragile."

Michael scoffed. "Please. You've spent more time at elite parties with a slew of bodyguards who fight off any danger."

"And you with a press badge around your neck isn't real danger either."

Michael bristled, heat rising in his eyes. "You'd be surprised, Simon. Not every truth gets printed. Some of us dig deeper into things than the headlines state."

Jayda stepped between them before fists could fly. "Enough. This isn't about family squabbles. Simon, go back to your family. I don't want to explain to them if something happens to you."

"Thanks a lot, Jayda. I thought we had something going between us." Simon's mouth twisted in anger and offense. "But fine. Don't say I didn't offer my help." He stormed off, disappearing into the crowd.

Jayda swallowed the guilt rising in her throat. She liked Simon but not romantically. She also knew she was using him to make Michael angry. Not her best moment. But now wasn't the time to rectify her actions.

"Time's ticking. We have less than four hours to figure out who Veronica Carlisle is and why men are willing to kill me over her pictures and papers."

Michael placed a hand on her elbow, gentle but firm. "Come on. We've got work to do."

Their first stop was a squat, windowless building tucked off a quieter street. The brass plaque read *United States Marshals Service*. Michael had made a call earlier—one of his contacts had arranged a meeting. Now they were here to see if the marshal could shed light on Veronica Carlisle.

Inside, the receptionist led them down a hallway lined with faded flags and framed commendations. The air smelled faintly of coffee and paper, and finally, they were ushered into a private office where a man in his late fifties sat behind a desk, typing. His nameplate read *Gerald Meeks.*

He looked up, his expression guarded. "Mr. Blair? And Ms.—"

"Simone," Jayda said quickly with her best lawyer voice.

Michael placed the documents on the desk. "This is what we came about. Can you tell us anything about this woman and why people are willing to kill for these papers?"

Meeks flipped through the documents, then tapped the photo of Veronica Carlisle. His brow furrowed as he typed on his computer keyboard. The silence stretched until finally he asked, "What's this for?"

Jayda exchanged a glance with Michael. "Men are after this information. They've already tried to kill me for it. Whoever she is, they want her badly."

Meeks leaned back, eyes unreadable. "She's already dead."

Jayda's stomach lurched. "What do you mean?"

"I mean Veronica Carlisle no longer exists," he said flatly. "Rest assured—there's nothing in these documents that would lead them anywhere."

His eyes said something different. He wasn't being forthright—she studied him closely, looking for the signs. He was good, but not perfect.

Michael pressed, "Then why the hunt?"

"Because," Meeks said, his tone sharpening, "they'll kill you before they realize the information is worthless."

The words chilled Jayda to the core. He was right. By the time those men learned the truth, she'd already be dead.

"Is there anything else you need?" Gerald asked.

"No, that's all." Jayda stood. She doubted he would share anyway.

They thanked him, though unease gnawed at Jayda's

insides. She gathered her bag and headed for the door, heart racing. Halfway down the hall, she froze.

Her phone. She'd left it on his desk.

"I'll be right back," she told Michael. She stepped up to the closed office door. Just as she was about to knock, Meeks's voice filtered out.

His voice was low and curt, talking to someone, "Follow them."

Jayda's blood ran cold. She backed away, leaving her phone behind, then darted down the hall.

She grabbed Michael's arm and whispered, "Run."

Thankfully, he didn't ask questions and led the way back through the building. They bolted out onto the street, the cold air hitting their lungs like knives. Jayda tugged Michael toward an alley. "We need to separate. It'll buy us time. Meet back at dinner."

Michael shook his head, breath puffing white in the air. "No, we stick together—"

But Jayda slipped free, heart hammering, sprinting down the narrow alley. Simon had been right. She led Michael right into danger. *God, let nothing happen to him. I never wanted him to be harmed.*

The prayer felt all wrong. Not because of her plea. She meant every word. Michael had been a nuisance to her for as long as she'd known him, but she didn't want him killed or even hurt. The prayer felt all wrong because she had never bothered God before for anything. She'd learned long ago that she was on her own. She didn't need anybody.

But this prayer was for Michael. *Lord, keep him safe.* She would take care of herself.

Jayda reached inside her coat pocket and felt the pink jewels around her stun gun. The moment she knew she wasn't alone in this alley, she held it at the ready.

She whirled around, and there—emerging from a doorway

—was the man from the train. The same one who had tried to break into her cabin.

The one with the hit-list.

His eyes locked on hers with a smile that said, "Game over."

She set off on a run straight at him, catching him by surprise. But she wasn't fast enough for a hitman, and in the blink of an eye, her weapon was turned on her.

Michael's heart slammed into his ribs with worry. He ran block to block, alley to alley. One moment Jayda was running beside him, and the next she was gone. The woman didn't understand the definition of family. She rejected every act of help his family offered and now this. Why did she think she had to face every obstacle alone? All questions he would demand answers for...after he found her.

But then had he ever offered her his help in any way? Did he ever treat her like family?

The answer to that question nearly caused him to stumble. She had no reason to trust him at all, and he had no right to ask her to. He wrote articles on peace deals but hadn't made peace in his own home.

Why? What had been the point? Had he really been jealous of her? Or was there something else he never wanted to face?

Michael turned the corner of the next block and stopped cold. The two men he'd seen chasing Jayda at the Penn Station platform stood dead ahead also looking down alleys. Jayda had thought she was drawing the men away from them, but she had no idea they'd closed off her escape before she even started running.

"Over here!" he shouted, his voice cutting across the street.

He raised his hand as if in surrender. "You're looking for me, right?"

The men pivoted, eyes narrowing, and one of them barked something into a radio clipped beneath his coat. A sick weight dropped into Michael's gut. Not just two of them. There were more.

And Jayda was alone to face them.

When the men sped his way, Michael forced his body to move, charging left down a side street lined with Christmas lights strung overhead, casting red hues in his path. The men followed, boots slapping the pavement behind him. A street performer dressed as an elf paused mid-bell jingle to gape as Michael tore past.

He led the men into the maze of holiday stalls. The Christkindlmarket. Glühwein steamed from mugs, wafting scents of cinnamon and cloves his way. Vendors hawked hand-carved ornaments, nutcrackers, and candied nuts. Michael took a right then a left then another left, pausing behind a sign for gingerbread. Two children gleefully bought giant cookies with bright red smiles, oblivious to the two killers weaving through the crowd behind them.

But a diversion wasn't a diversion when the enemy had already planned the board. Michael had drawn some heat away from Jayda—but not all of it. She was somewhere in these streets fighting for her life.

He wove through the market, shoving through the crowd, hoping the men didn't spot him. The maze had two more rows to go. His investigative brain, usually razor-sharp under pressure, fuzzed with one thought: *Jayda is in danger.*

The men stepped out, one from the right and one from the left. They blocked him behind a row of wreath stalls, half-hidden in the glow of white lights. One man lunged, reaching inside his coat. Michael reacted without thinking—fist slamming into his jaw. The man reeled, colliding with a stack of crates, and evergreen wreaths tumbled everywhere, pine needles flying like shrapnel.

The second man came at him harder, swinging low. Michael dodged, took a punch to the ribs, and grunted. He wasn't green. He'd been in tight spots chasing cartel money and human traffickers, but these men weren't street thugs. They were professionals—trained, disciplined and dangerous.

Michael kicked the first man square in the knee when he tried to rise. The crack was audible. His scream louder. One down. But the second had a knife now, the glint catching the Christmas lights above.

Michael ducked as the blade swiped, the air whooshing past his face. He grabbed a string of twinkling lights from the stall and yanked. With the wire tangled around the man's wrist, the knife clattered to the ground.

Michael punched him once, twice, until the man slumped.

Chest heaving, he stumbled backward, adrenaline flooding him. The wreath vendor screamed at him that he was calling the cops.

"Do it!" Michael replied.

Somewhere nearby, carolers sang *O Holy Night*. The contrast made bile rise in his throat. He staggered back to the streets and alleys. Each of them empty.

No Jayda.

Panic iced his veins.

"Jayda!"

Nothing.

He ran, scanning alleys, crowds, every shadow. She was gone. They'd taken her, or she was still cornered. Either way, time was running out.

He shoved through a group of photographer elves with their Santa. Children gathered to meet the big guy, and here Michael was, leading danger to them. For one sharp second he thought of Simon's words—*What about Michael's safety?*—

and almost laughed bitterly. He'd thrown himself into this willingly. And now innocent people could pay for his choices.

Michael spun in the street, frantic, needing to separate from the crowds. Then—a strange movement far past the ice rink. A tall man dragged another person toward the glow of the winter fairground. The other person slumped in the crook of his arm. A set of black curls moved Michael's feet in their direction.

Jayda.

There were masses of people between them.

Michael bolted, and sharp cold air burned his throat. The Chicago air had teeth tonight—winter biting deep and clinging to the lining of his lungs. Snowflakes drifted lazily under the strings of Christmas lights crisscrossing Millennium Park, painting the scene deceptively festive when a woman was being kidnapped. Couples twirled hand in hand on the ice rink. Children shrieked with joy as they clung to their parents and learned to skate. The music from a brass quartet echoed under the towering Christmas tree nearby.

A scene of holiday perfection.

Except Jayda barely moved in the man's grip. She appeared lifeless.

Michael shoved through the crowd at the edge of the rink. The fastest way to them would be to cross the rink. His throat tightened. He couldn't shout, not yet. Panic would spread, and panic meant Jayda could get hurt before he reached her. He needed to get across the ice and cut the man off from leaving the park.

Michael shoved a teenager aside, muttering an apology, and vaulted onto the ice in his boots. Bad idea. His feet shot out as if he'd just stepped on a banana peel. He hit the ice flat on his back, the cold jolting straight through his spine.

Great. Smooth. Real heroic.

Gritting his teeth, he scrambled upright, wobbling like a

newborn deer. His leather boots had zero grip on sheer ice. The Christmas carols booming over the speakers made a mockery of his desperate stagger. People laughed. A little girl zipped past him with the grace of an Olympian, giggling, "You're supposed to wear skates!"

"Yeah, thanks for the tip," he muttered, eyes locked on Jayda.

She was halfway to the gate now. The man leaned in close, speaking in her ear. Her expression was set tight, but her eyes darted all around her—she was conscious. So why wasn't she fighting the man?

"I'm here," Michael whispered, though she couldn't hear him. His chest burned as he forced himself forward. Every step was a battle between balance and disaster. He slipped once, twice—his arms windmilling wildly—but each fall only made him angrier.

Come on. Hurry up. Maybe this wasn't the fastest way across.

Finally, he gave up his dignity altogether. He dropped into a half-crouch, using the palms of his hands to push off the ice, sliding forward in awkward spurts. He must've looked like a malfunctioning seal, but it got him closer.

Then Jayda's head turned. Her eyes met his across the rink. For an instant, fear flickered into relief. Then her captor noticed too.

The man's free hand went for his pocket, then steel glinted. A knife.

"Jayda!" Michael bellowed, his voice cutting through the Christmas music.

Heads turned. A few gasps rippled across the crowd. The man jerked Jayda toward the park's exit, moving faster now. Michael's stomach knotted—he'd never make it at this pace.

He jumped back to his feet and sprinted—or the ice-booted version of sprinting—straight toward the railing and launched himself. His knee slammed into the barrier, pain jolting up his leg, but adrenaline numbed it. He vaulted over, landing hard on the walkway just as the man dragged Jayda into the shadows beyond the rink.

"Let her go!" Michael roared, charging, closing the gap between them.

The man turned to face him, the knife pressed to Jayda's ribs. Her captor's voice was low and cold. "Stay back, or she bleeds."

Michael froze, chest heaving. His fists clenched helplessly. Every instinct screamed to tackle the guy, but he couldn't risk it—not with the blade at her side.

Jayda's gaze flicked to him. Wide. Afraid. But beneath the fear... something sharp. Calculating. One leg moved and then the other, but it buckled right away.

And then it hit him. She'd been tasered, probably with her own stun gun. He locked his gaze on her, drilling into her eyes the support to try again. A memory came to his mind. A much younger Jayda, wiry and furious, flooring him in Ginny and Ed's living room after he'd teased her too far. A move she'd pulled from God knows where—one second he'd been laughing, the next he was staring at the ceiling with her knee in his chest.

He remembered exactly how she'd done it.

"Jayda," he said, steadying his voice. "Remember the move. The one you used on me once."

Her brows flicked. She knew.

He nodded once for her to do it.

Jayda tested her legs again, this time more stable.

The man sneered, confused at their conversation. The time gave Jayda what she needed.

In the next second, she twisted hard, slamming her heel down on his instep. The man hissed, knife jerking just enough. Jayda bent low, grabbed his wrist, and pivoted—using his own momentum against him. The same move she'd used on Michael years ago.

The man hit the pavement with a grunt, knife clattering free.

"Good girl," Michael said, lunging for the weapon. He kicked the blade away and drove his fist into the man's jaw. Bone cracked under his knuckles. The man went slack, groaning.

Michael hauled Jayda upright. "You okay?"

Her breath puffed white, shaky but defiant. "Yeah. Now, I am. But I might still need you to hold me up."

He chuckled. "Your stun gun?"

She offered a wobbly smile with a little chagrin. "Thanks for the reminder...about the move."

"Don't mention it."

But their relief lasted only a heartbeat. When they turned, two more men stepped from the shadows, a feral expression on their faces. Both wore dark coats, their hands resting casually inside—concealing weapons, no doubt.

Michael shoved Jayda slightly behind him, his pulse hammering. "You want her, you'll have to go through me."

The first man shook his head almost sadly. "You don't understand. This isn't about you. Walk away, and maybe we'll let you keep breathing."

Michael wasn't about to wait for them to make a move. But Jayda wasn't ready to run. He did the only thing he could, scooping her up to cradle her, and sprinting back to the glow of the Christmas bazaar. The police would have hopefully arrived already. He weaved through stalls but this time remembered a cab parked on the right side of the fair.

At last, they burst out onto Michigan Avenue, where the taxi still waited at the curb, the driver eating a donut.

They'd made it. Barely.

Michael opened the rear door and tossed Jayda inside, both of them collapsing into the seat.

"Go!" he yelled, his jaw tight, scanning the sidewalks. The men hadn't made it through...or made other plans to cut them off somewhere else.

The driver took to the streets with precision and speed, but Michael had to be ready for an ambush at any second.

These men weren't done. Not by a long shot.

Seven

Jayda stepped through the double doors into the Santa Village lodge. The warmth cocooned her like a blanket after the icy chaos outside. Her nerves still trembled from her electrical stun gun experience. Michael must have noticed because he put his hand on her back, which was so out of his character.

"You're here!" Ginny shouted from the other end of the hotel lobby that looked like the North Pole. Candles twinkled on every table. Strings of garland looped across the beams of the high timbered ceiling. A giant Christmas tree soared in the corner, its ornaments glittering in soft gold and red.

Jayda tried to slow her pulse with deep breaths. Her heart rate hadn't slowed since she had felt the man's arm around her throat and the bite of his knife at her side. The images burned like a brand, but she pasted on a Christmas cheer smile for Ginny.

Fake calm. She'd lived her life with it, hadn't she? When foster parents fought, when teachers labeled her trouble, when Michael used to look at her with that cutting disdain back in their teenage years. If she'd learned one survival skill, it was pretending she was fine.

Ginny rushed forward, her holiday sweater blazing with sequined poinsettias. She enveloped Jayda in a hug so genuine it made Jayda's throat ache. Then Ginny reached for Michael, hugging him fiercely too.

"Oh, thank heavens you're both here. I was so worried something might separate us. But we're all here and safe."

Safe. The word felt foreign. But Jayda nodded even though it was a lie.

Behind Ginny, Ed stood from his chair by the fireplace, putting the boys down from his lap. He strode up, broad-shouldered, cheeks red from the flames. He gave Michael a nod. "Glad to see you kept your word."

"Of course," Michael said, his voice rougher than usual. He looked away from his father with a tick in his jaw that caused Jayda to pause in wonder. Had she ever noticed the disconnect between father and son? What caused it?

Before she could figure it out, the twins barreled into Jayda like twin snowballs. Timmy and Tyler, identical in red plaid shirts and jeans, their curls fresh and clean.

"Did Ginny give you a bubble bath?" Jayda asked, tweaking their noses.

"Yes!" they answered in unison.

"She gives the best bubble baths. The bubbles overflow right out of the tub." Jayda smiled with the boys, focusing on settling her heart rate into a peaceful rhythm.

"Did Santa come yet?" Timmy demanded.

"He'll be here soon," Ginny said. "But only if you're good."

"I'm good," Tyler whined.

Jayda crouched so she was eye level, bopping their noses. "He wouldn't miss you two. And I'm sure he's excited to meet you."

The boys squealed and dashed toward the stage where a chair draped in red velvet waited, empty for now.

The fake calm nearly slipped. Jayda's stomach twisted, remembering the danger still prowling outside. The men could still be looking for her, waiting to make another move. But for the boys' sake, for Ginny's sake, she stood strong, looking carefree. Jayda took her seat beside Michael, and when he reached under the table to take her hand to squeeze, she nearly let the façade slip. Tears pricked her eyes, forcing her chin down to push them away.

The room buzzed with chatter around her as her mind whirled with what might have happened to her today. No amount of street smarts could have saved her.

Jayda turned to Michael and whispered, "I'm sorry I brought you into this today. I shouldn't have done that. Your family doesn't deserve to lose you because of me. And they could have today. They still could."

"And what about you? They don't deserve to lose you either."

"It's not the same, and you know it."

"What are you two whispering about down there?" Ginny called, passing plates of roast beef and potatoes to the twins. The sound of her questioning voice made Jayda flinch.

Jayda's mouth went dry, unsure of what to say. She had to think of something.

Suddenly, Michael jumped in and replied, "Sorry, Mom, we actually ate while we were out. We were just saying we aren't very hungry."

Ginny pouted, but before she could scold them for ruining their dinner, Santa's hearty *ho-ho-ho* filtered into the dining room.

"Santa! Santa's here!" Timmy shouted and pushed back his chair.

"Oh, no you don't," Ginny said, all focus on the twins again to keep them seated.

Jayda exhaled in relief. Michael thwarted Ginny's curiosity for now, but when Jayda glanced at him, he was scanning the exits, jaw set, eyes sharp. She hadn't thought about how he was feeling, only her own nerves.

The realization lodged like a splinter. He had nearly been killed tonight because of her.

What would she have said to Ginny and Ed if something had happened to Michael?

A sudden cheer rose from the children clustered near the stage. The big moment had arrived.

The man in the red suit swept in, his beard white as snow, bells jingling with each step. The lodge erupted in applause. Children squealed and rushed forward. Even the adults clapped and laughed as though their own childhoods had just walked through the door.

Timmy and Tyler froze. The boys who had been bouncing in their seats minutes earlier now clung to Ginny's sleeves, eyes wide with awe.

"He's...big," Timmy whispered.

"I'm scared," Tyler added.

They were practically trembling with trepidation. Jayda smiled at their expressions. Then Michael pushed back and stood, making his way to the twins. He crouched beside them.

"Hey. You know what? Santa's probably nervous too. Meeting you guys? That's a big deal for him."

The boys blinked at him.

"You really think so?" Timmy asked.

Michael nodded. "Absolutely. So maybe you should go shake his hand. Just a handshake. Let him know you're not scary."

Slowly, Tyler hopped down and slipped his hand into

Michael's. Timmy followed. And with Michael leading, they walked up to Santa.

Jayda's breath caught as she watched. Michael knelt, spoke quietly, and encouraged them. He didn't push, didn't tease. Just steady encouragement until, at last, both boys extended trembling hands to Santa. Soon the twins were whispering their Christmas wishes into his ear.

It was the first time Jayda had ever seen Michael this way. Gentle. Patient. Caring.

Had she been wrong about him all these years?

She wanted to reject the idea, to cling to her old view of him—the arrogant boy, the dismissive foster brother. But the evidence was standing right in front of her. Michael had put his life on the line for her. And now, here he was, guiding two frightened little boys into joy.

Her throat tightened.

"Family picture!" Ginny called suddenly. "Everyone, come on!"

Chairs scraped as the Blairs gathered near the tree with Santa. And before Jayda knew it, Ginny had tugged her into the lineup—right beside Michael.

"Perfect," Ginny declared, stepping up beside her husband.

Jayda stiffened, feeling too close. She inched sideways to give him space—and herself. Then she felt his hand slip into hers and squeeze.

Her pulse stuttered.

It felt so right. But that couldn't be right.

She pulled her hand free just as the photographer snapped the shot. The flash burst across her vision, and she turned to look at him, more stunned by the way she was feeling than the bright light.

Neither of them smiled, only stared at each other. Something between them had changed that day. Is this what a life-

or-death situation did to people? All she wanted to do was let him hold her again.

The shocking thought caused her to step away, putting space between them.

Then Simon appeared at her side.

"Jayda," he said as the family began to disperse. "Train's leaving soon. Want me to walk you back to the station?"

Jayda hesitated. She didn't dare look at Michael. She couldn't bear the weight of his eyes on her, not after what had just passed between them.

So she turned to Simon and slid her hand through his looped arm. "Yes," she said. "I'd like that very much."

They made their way to the exit while Christmas music followed them out, bright and merry, but it felt like a mockery to how she was feeling—like a traitor.

Michael had never been good at pretending, and he wasn't about to pretend everything between him and Jayda hadn't changed today.

For years, their relationship had been built on teasing that went too far. A constant competition to prove who could stand taller in the house his parents had made for both of them. He'd always told himself it was sibling rivalry, nothing more.

But they weren't siblings. Not really.

And the way his chest had nearly torn apart watching her walk out of the lodge with Simon—this feeling had nothing to do with sibling anything.

The night air bit against his skin as they moved in a cheerful little herd. Ginny linked arms with Ed, the twins skipping ahead, their laughter rising above the jingle of bells from a street performer. Lights sparkled from every lamppost. Holiday music drifted from shop doors as crowds hurried home with packages.

Michael tried to fix his eyes on the normalcy of it all. Pretend the world hadn't tilted on its axis tonight. Pretend men weren't hunting them, that Jayda hadn't nearly been killed in his arms. Pretend his heart wasn't battering itself against his ribs.

"Michael."

His mother's voice cut gently into his thoughts. Ginny had slowed, letting the others walk ahead. She slipped her gloved hand through his arm, her head tilting toward him.

"You've been quiet tonight."

He forced a shrug. "Long day."

She studied him with her all-knowing mother's gaze, the kind that never missed a beat. "You and Jayda...something feels different."

Michael's heart stuttered. He kept his eyes straight ahead, on the glowing arch of the station entrance. "Different how?"

"I don't know." Ginny's tone was sweet, almost teasing, but edged with intuition. "For years it was bickering, like cats and dogs. Now, tonight, I saw something else. Something friendlier."

He swallowed hard. He couldn't tell her. Couldn't tell her they had been running from men with knives, couldn't tell her that his pulse had nearly stopped when he thought Jayda might be dead. Couldn't tell her the truth—that he didn't know where the line between him and his old foster sister had been moved or maybe even erased.

"Don't read too much into it," he managed. "Jayda and I... we've both grown up. That's all."

Ginny gave him a knowing smile, but she didn't press. She never did when he wasn't ready. Instead, she patted his arm and said, "It does a mother's heart well to see her children getting along." Then she hurried forward to catch up with the twins, who were already darting up the marble steps of Union Station.

Michael exhaled with relief while keeping a lookout for any unwanted passengers. The train was warm with no sign of the men. Michael kept close behind his family as they found their seats. The twins immediately began whispering about Santa finding them even on a train. Ginny spread a blanket across their laps. Ed disappeared in search of coffee.

But Jayda wasn't with them.

Michael scanned the next car, his pulse already climbing. He spotted her at last—sitting in the dining car with Simon.

They leaned close across the table, their heads nearly touching. Jayda's hands were folded in front of her, her expression guarded, but her attention fixed on Simon. And Simon looked every bit the confident, smooth-talking man Michael had always distrusted.

Michael crossed over to the next train before he could stop himself. His boots thudded against the floor, his breath tight in his chest.

As soon as he reached them, Jayda and Simon fell quiet.

Simon leaned back in his seat, his mouth tugging in something that wasn't quite a smile. "Relax, Mike. Jayda's filled me in on what went down."

Michael's gut clenched. He darted a glance around the car. He turned back to Simon, his voice low and dangerous. "This doesn't leave this table."

Simon shrugged as though it didn't matter. He stood, straightening his coat. Then he reached out his hand toward Jayda. "Don't worry. I'll keep watch over her."

Jayda winced, standing firm. "I don't want help from either of you. It's too dangerous. I'm the one who tasered the guy, remember? I handled it. And I'll keep handling it."

Michael opened his mouth to tell her to forget it, not happening, but she raised her hand to stop him.

Jayda's voice dropped. "I'm getting off this train. I'm not dragging your family into this. I could never forgive myself if something happened to any of you...to the twins. They deserve a safe home, a family...something I didn't have until—"

She cut herself short.

Michael's stomach lurched. She should have said *Until Ginny and Ed took me in.* She should have felt safe and welcome in their home. His parents had made her family. But him? He had made her feel like an intruder.

The guilt hit him like a fist.

Jayda straightened abruptly, as though shutting the thought down before she spoke the truth. "I'll leave without saying goodbye. Don't tell Ginny and Ed until after the train leaves Chicago. Please."

Simon frowned. "Where will you go?"

She frowned. "I don't know. I'll figure it out. I'll survive. Hide out for a while."

Michael's throat closed.

Her graduation, her plans—everything she'd worked toward—suspended in an instant. She was throwing it away to protect his family.

Simon reached into his coat and pulled out the wad of cash he'd flashed a few days before. He pressed it into her hand. "Take this."

Jayda blinked, startled. "Simon—"

"Don't argue," he said firmly.

Michael stood stunned. He'd spent so long distrusting Simon, writing him off as arrogant and reckless. But this? This was generosity and selfless. Something Michael hadn't expected. Perhaps Simon wasn't the one he should have worried about taking advantage of Jayda. Maybe it was himself.

And now, she was walking off this train...and out of his life, possibly never to see her again.

He deserved nothing less.

Panic arose in his chest at the sight of her heading to the end of the car and out the sliding door. She slipped out and stepped off the car.

Michael's body moved before his brain could. He followed, heart hammering as she walked down the platform. Through the window, he caught a last glimpse of her coat vanishing down the walk.

And then she was gone.

He reached the end of the car just as the sound of the conductor's whistle pierced the air. The train shuddered and then lurched forward.

"Jayda!"

Michael's voice tore from his throat. He sprinted, shoving past passengers, racing to the exit and outside. The platform was already sliding by in a blur.

He leapt, not even thinking twice.

For one sickening second, he was flying. Then, his hands slammed against the edge of the platform, his body dangling. His boots scraped the ground. He hauled himself up with a grunt, chest heaving, eyes scanning desperately.

"Jayda! Wait!"

His voice echoed through the station, swallowed by the sound of the moving train. He pushed forward, running into the night.

"Jayda!" he called again as the train swept past them, leaving them behind.

She had stopped under a lamplight, her figure a dark silhouette against the golden glow. For a moment she looked like something out of a dream, her coat billowing in the winter wind.

Michael ran to her, closing the distance. His hands found her forearms, gripping her. "I won't let you do this alone. Do you hear me? I would never forgive myself. Just like you'd never forgive yourself for staying. Well, I can't stand by and do nothing either."

Her eyes glistened in the light. "Why, Michael? Why are you doing this?"

He hesitated. The answer burned in his throat, terrifying and raw.

At last, he shook his head. "Because I was wrong. I was wrong to treat you so horribly when you needed me most. You came to our house as a kid—you needed a friend. And I failed you." His grip tightened. "This is my chance to fix that. To make it up to you. I'm not letting another day go by with me standing on the sidelines while you fight alone."

For a moment, she just stared at him. Then, her arms wrapped around him, sudden and fierce. She buried her face against his chest, and the dam inside him broke.

He wrapped her tightly, pressing his chin to her hair. "You're not doing this alone," he whispered. "I won't leave your side."

She pulled back slowly, her eyes searching his.

He saw the war inside her, the battle between trust and fear. The part of her that longed to believe him and the part that still bore the scars of his rejection.

It hurt. God, it hurt.

Without another thought, he lowered his head, brushing his lips against hers. Gently at first. Just to let her know he was sorry. Just to promise he would never treat her the same.

But then she kissed him back, giving him her trust, and something inside him became clear. Jayda had always been important to him. Always. And now he couldn't hide it any longer.

He deepened the kiss, one hand sliding to her back,

pulling her closer, anchoring himself to the only thing in this moment that felt real and safe.

Until the crack of a gunshot split the night.

Eight

Gunfire cracked the night like an exploding firework, sharp and jarring, snapping Jayda back to the reality of the threat on her life.

She stumbled against Michael, her lips tingling, her breath caught somewhere between a laugh and a scream. They had kissed. She had kissed her archenemy.

And now, bullets were flying while the warmth of Michael's mouth on hers could still be felt. Nothing made sense.

"Run!" Michael's voice echoed in the night with urgency, his hand seizing hers before she could blink.

They bolted, boots pounding the icy pavement, weaving between lamppost shadows. The sting of cold air burned Jayda's lungs, but she didn't dare slow. Trouble had found them again. She should've been annoyed that Michael had jumped from the train after her. She should've snapped at him for interfering.

But she wasn't annoyed. She was grateful.

As bullets sparked against a metal trash can just feet away,

Jayda realized she had never in her life been so glad not to be alone.

Michael pulled her toward the cover of a stone archway, his arm instinctively braced against her back as another shot cracked in the distance. The sound ricocheted through the city square, bouncing off windows and brick walls, impossible to pinpoint.

Her pulse thundered. "Where is he?"

Michael shook his head, his expression fiercely focused. His other hand rested against the bricks, shielding her with his body. His eyes darted across the street. "I don't know. Keep moving."

They sprinted again, this time dodging a row of iron benches and ducking behind a pillar wrapped in garland and twinkling lights. The absurdity hit her then—how something as beautiful as Christmas decorations could become cover in a street chase.

A shot rang out, splintering the wooden frame of a storefront across the street. Jayda flinched, clutching Michael's hand tighter.

The strength of his grip startled her. She had never held someone's hand in desperation like this. Not since she was a child clinging to her mother's before sickness tore them apart. Independence had been her armor. Needing no one had been her mantra.

Yet here she was, tethered to Michael Blair—the boy she used to despise, the man she thought still resented her—and all she wanted was not to let go.

They cut a sharp turn, lungs burning, legs aching. Jayda thought her chest might split open when suddenly a sound rose ahead that froze her in place.

Singing.

She blinked in disbelief.

A group of bundled carolers stood in the glow of a corner

streetlamp, their voices lifted in soft harmony. The melody floated like fragile glass over the chaos, wrapping the night in calm.

"Silent night, holy night..." they sang.

Michael's hand tightened on hers, slowing their run. He pulled her back against the wall, opposite the carolers. His chest heaved against her shoulder as he whispered, "We can't lead him toward them."

Jayda nodded quickly, pressing herself into the shadows beside him. They crouched, letting the music mask their ragged breathing.

The gunfire stopped.

Jayda's ears strained against the silence. Only the carolers sang, their breath visible in white puffs, their faces lit with the candles they held. The contrast was surreal—death and danger only a heartbeat away, yet here was peace.

It was almost as though even their pursuer respected the moment.

Her shoulders dropped an inch, the tightness in her chest loosening as the voices wove around them. For the first time since the shots began, Jayda breathed deeply.

Michael leaned closer, his whisper brushing her ear. "Funny how even a shooter has to pause for Christmas."

A laugh bubbled up in her throat, too breathless to release. She turned slightly, her gaze catching the flicker of wonder in his eyes. "You think that's what this is? Holiday respect?"

"I think..." His voice softened. "I've never paid the season much thought before. Maybe I should have."

She swallowed, her throat tight at his confession. She wasn't supposed to feel anything for him—least of all this strange ache at his honesty.

"My mom..." Jayda's voice trembled, but she pushed through. "She made Christmas matter, even when we had nothing. Even if it was just paper snowflakes and cookies from ingredients she scraped together. She made it feel special."

Michael's jaw worked, his eyes on the carolers. "I'm glad to hear that. I'm sorry I never asked before. I was just angry that you rejected my mom's attempts."

Guilt stabbed her chest, sharp and unexpected. Ginny. Sweet, persistent Ginny, who had tried to make Christmas special too, who Jayda had kept at arm's length. "I never let myself enjoy it with Ginny. It felt like cheating on my mom. Like if I let myself belong to her family, I'd forget my real one."

Michael's gaze flicked to her. His voice was low. "I humored my mom. But if I'm being honest—I've been ungrateful. For all she's done."

Jayda blinked, the weight of realization settling over her like the hush of snow. "We left her behind and this silly train trip she loved putting together. We just...left."

The song shifted, the carolers' voices rising in cheerful tempo as they moved on, singing, *"We wish you a merry Christmas..."*

The feeling changed instantly, from peace to war. Michael straightened, scanning the street again.

Jayda's chest thudded with urgency. "We have to get back on that train before Ginny realizes we're gone."

Michael nodded. "She will be heartbroken."

"But how will we get to the next stop? It's Missouri."

"Nearest rental car's three blocks," he said, checking his phone, thumb quick over the screen.

Jayda seized his hand, no hesitation this time. "Let's move. Together." And before fear could stop her, she leaned up and kissed him quickly. Maybe out of reassurance that she wasn't doing this alone, or maybe out of a need she wasn't ready to dissect.

His stunned inhale brushed her cheek. His eyes burned

into hers, sparking with determination. "When this is over, we need to talk."

"*If* we make it."

He kissed her back. "Oh, we'll make it. I'll make sure we do."

The rental car place was smaller than Michael expected, tucked in at the edge of the bus terminal lot like an afterthought. Its neon sign flickered against the evening sky, the glow barely cutting through the thick, falling snowflakes. Inside, the clerk looked half-asleep, leaning on the counter with a weariness that said he'd rather be anywhere else than renting out cars on Christmas week.

Michael filled out the paperwork, his drivers license sliding across the counter with hands that he willed to look steady. But the adrenaline still hummed from earlier, every nerve on edge. Jayda stood just behind him, silent, her arms folded tight across her chest, her eyes flicked to the windows. The shooter was still out there, tracking them.

"Lucky day," the clerk muttered, pushing a single key across the counter. "One left. Small hatchback."

Michael lifted an eyebrow. "Just one? Anything...faster?"

The clerk shrugged. "Nope. It's Christmas week. You want it or not? Folks have been snatching them up before the storm gets bad."

Michael glanced at Jayda. She gave the smallest nod. They didn't have options. He took the key.

The hatchback sat under a blanket of snow in the lot's corner, barely visible until they trudged up to it. Michael brushed off the windshield with the side of his arm, revealing a car that looked more suited to grocery runs than mountain roads. They might not catch the train until Denver if they didn't get driving. He heard Jayda's low exhale behind him.

"Cozy," she said, voice dry.

Michael opened the driver's side door with a creak. "If cozy's another word for impractical in a snowstorm."

The car sputtered to life on the third turn of the key. The heater groaned before finally pushing out a weak stream of lukewarm air. Michael adjusted the mirrors, gave the wheel a testing grip, and pulled out of the lot.

The road stretched dark ahead of them, snowflakes swirling under the beams of the headlights. He could feel the tires slipping now and again, struggling to grip. The weight of catching the train pressed down heavy.

For a while, silence filled the compact car, broken only by the windshield wipers fighting against the snow. Michael kept his eyes on the road, but his awareness stayed trained on the woman beside him. He could feel her restless energy—like she was holding her breath.

Then, out of nowhere, she laughed.

It startled him enough that his grip tightened on the wheel. "What?" he asked, his voice sharper than he intended. "What's so funny?"

She shook her head, still laughing softly, a sound both strange and startling in the tense quiet. "I was just thinking...if someone asked me a week ago if I'd be in a car with Michael Blair, of all people, during a snowstorm, chasing after his family to catch a train..." She pressed her gloved hand to her mouth to stifle another laugh. "I'd have told them they were out of their minds."

Michael cut her a quick look, surprised by the brightness in her eyes. He hadn't realized how much he needed to see it—her laughing, even at his expense. It cracked through the fear like a match struck in darkness.

"You think this is funny?" he said, but his tone softened, teasing.

"I think," she said, still grinning, "this must be some kind of Christmas miracle. You and I in this car, together."

Warmth spread through him that had nothing to do with the heater kicking in. He nodded, turning his attention back to the snowy road. "Miracle's one word for it."

Her laughter faded into a smile, and she leaned back against the seat, her breath fogging faintly in the cool air of the cabin. For the first time since this whole thing started, Michael felt something ease inside him. They were still being followed, still in danger, still driving through a snowstorm in a car that wasn't built for it—but sitting next to her, it didn't feel quite as impossible.

He focused on the road, but his thoughts wandered. His boss was expecting a story before Christmas Eve. Something nostalgic. Families coming together for the holidays. Heartwarming copy that readers could sip cocoa over. But what would he think if Michael delivered something different—raw, urgent, a story about family that wasn't tied up with bows and candlelight but with grit and sacrifice? A story about choosing to be together, no matter the cost?

The idea sparked something inside him, something that pushed against the weight he carried. But he kept it to himself. The last thing Jayda needed was to think he was doing all this for a headline. He was doing it because...well, because he cared.

Snow thickened, swirling faster. Michael leaned forward slightly, eyes narrowing as he scanned the road ahead. His hands tightened on the wheel. He could feel the car shudder under him, straining.

Then headlights flared in the mirror.

He stiffened at the sight of a vehicle behind them, closing in too fast.

Jayda noticed immediately. Her head snapped toward the side mirror, her posture going rigid. "Michael..."

"I see it," he said, forcing calm into his tone even as adrenaline spiked through him.

The headlights grew brighter, closer. The other vehicle's engine roared, tires crunching over snow and ice. Michael kept their hatchback steady, hands tight, eyes darting to the narrow shoulders of the road. Snowbanks rose high on either side. No room. No escape.

The vehicle swerved, nudging too close. Gunshots pierced the night.

"Michael!" Jayda's voice sharpened with fear.

A loud pop jolted the car violently, forcing it toward the snowbank. The wheel fought in his hands. The tires skidded, screaming against the ice.

Michael gritted his teeth, muscles straining as he tried to hold them steady, but momentum was against him. The hatchback lurched sideways, the headlights cutting wild arcs across the snow.

Jayda braced herself against the dash, eyes wide, lips parted in a silent scream.

And then—

The world tilted.

The car slid off the road, crunching into the bank with a bone-jarring slam. The engine sputtered and died.

For a moment, silence. Only the sound of their ragged breathing.

Michael's hands still gripped the wheel, knuckles aching. His chest heaved, heart pounding in his ears. Slowly, he turned his head toward Jayda.

"You okay?" he asked, voice rough.

She nodded quickly, but her eyes were still wide, adrenaline shining there. "I think so. You?"

"I'm fine," he said, though his pulse screamed otherwise.

He forced his hands off the wheel, flexing fingers that still trembled. "We're off the road."

Jayda turned to look out her window. Snow pressed up against the glass, the world outside dark and distorted. She drew a sharp breath. "They're still out there. But if we stay here, we'll freeze to death."

Michael searched the street above. Headlights glowed on the road above, lingering for a beat before sliding away into the storm.

But for how long until they circled back to finish them?

Michael exhaled hard. They were being hunted. And the night was only beginning.

Nine

Snowflakes stung Jayda's cheeks as the sharp bite of the wind assaulted her. The hatchback sat half-buried at the side of the road, its hazard lights winking weakly through the blizzard. The shot-out tire had forced them off, the other car speeding away like a predator knowing its prey couldn't run. Jayda's heart pounded so hard she was sure Michael could hear it.

"They're going to come back," she whispered, scanning the white haze of the storm, every shadow a threat, every gust of wind sounding like an engine drawing near.

Michael pressed close, his hand finding her elbow. "I know. Which is why we can't stay here." His voice was firm, calm in a way that helped anchor her spiraling thoughts. "Come on. We need to move."

Her boots crunched through the growing snowdrifts as they started down a narrow street branching away from the highway. The storm howled. Visibility shrank to only a few feet ahead. Jayda hugged her arms tight against her body, shivering not only from the cold but from the knowledge that whoever had shot their tire wasn't done. Whoever wanted

Veronica Carlisle silenced—and anyone standing in the way—wouldn't let a snowstorm stop them.

"Michael," she said, her voice breaking with the strain, "if they find us out here..."

"They won't," he interrupted, his hand brushing hers as they trudged forward together. "We'll find shelter first. Stay with me."

His confidence wasn't arrogance; it was conviction. Something in it seeped into her bones, warming her in a way the storm couldn't touch. She tightened her jaw and kept moving, focusing on the rhythm of her steps and the dark outline of houses beginning to take shape through the curtain of snow.

But before they reached the street of houses, a car rolled slowly down the road, its headlights cutting through the white squall. The tires crunched over the snow—too slow, too careful. Jayda's heart leapt into her throat.

"Hide," Michael ordered. He pulled her against the shadow of a two-story home, its windows dark, curtains drawn tight. The porch beckoned as a place to protect them from view. They ran up the stairs and pressed close against the wall.

The car crept past, the driver's face a blur behind the frost-laced windshield. The brake lights glowed red for one terrifying second, but then the car rolled on. Jayda held her breath until the glow disappeared into the snow.

Only then did Michael step back and knock firmly on the door of the dark house.

"Are you crazy?" she whispered harshly. "What if it's not safe?"

"It's safer than freezing out here," he said, his eyes locking on hers, steady. "Trust me, Jayda. Just trust me."

She wanted to argue, but her bones felt like ice, and every second outside put them closer to being hunted down or freezing to death. She swallowed her fear and stayed close to him as the sound of shuffling footsteps echoed from within.

A light flicked on, yellow and warm against the glass pane. The door opened to reveal an older man, gray hair tucked under a cap, lines etched deep into his face. His eyes narrowed, suspicious but not unkind.

"Can I help you folks?" he asked, his voice rough, like gravel.

Michael's hand hovered protectively near her back. "Sir, our car's got a flat. The storm's too bad to fix it on the road, and we don't have anywhere safe to go." His tone was polite but laced with urgency. "We were hoping...maybe you'd let us come in out of the cold for a while."

The old man studied them for a long beat, his gaze flicking to the road behind them, then back. Finally, he sighed, stepping aside. "Get in before you freeze solid."

Relief surged through Jayda as she stepped into the warmth of the house. The smell of wood smoke and old pine filled her nose, heat from a cast-iron stove wrapping around her frozen limbs. She almost sagged against the wall.

"I'm Chuck," the man said, closing the door behind them. He glanced between the two of them with a squint.

"I'm Michael Blair, and this is Jayda. Thank you so much, sir."

"Couple of young folks out in this mess—it's no good. Where you two headed?"

Michael answered before Jayda could. "Missouri. We were supposed to meet up with family, catch a train in Kansas City. But with the car..." he trailed off, rubbing the back of his neck.

Chuck's brow furrowed, then softened. "Train station, huh? I can take you there. Got a truck that'll handle this weather better than any car."

Jayda blinked. "You'd do that? Just...drive strangers through a snowstorm? It's at least six hours from here."

He shrugged, settling into a worn recliner near the stove to put his boots on. "Storm this bad, people look out for each other. Ain't no sense leaving you out there to freeze. Besides—" his lips twitched into a small smile—"I like a good drive in the snow."

Jayda exchanged a stunned glance with Michael. She could see the same surprise mirrored in his eyes but also gratitude.

"Thank you," Michael said sincerely. "That means more than you know."

Chuck waved him off. "Don't thank me yet. Roads are bad, and it'll take time. Can't guarantee you'll make your train, but I'll get you there and do my best."

The ride in Chuck's old truck was tight and cold. The cab was small, forcing the three of them close together on the bench seat, and the frosty air seeped through the seams despite the heater's best effort. Michael took the middle, Jayda by the door, and outside, the storm raged. Flakes whirled in chaotic bursts across the windshield. The wipers worked furiously to keep up.

Chuck hummed softly to himself, hands steady on the wheel, as though he'd driven through a hundred blizzards before.

Jayda tried to stay alert, but exhaustion clawed at her. Every muscle ached, her eyelids growing heavier with each passing mile. She felt the warmth of Michael's arm brushing hers, inviting her to sleep.

"You holding up?" he murmured, leaning close so only she could hear.

She nodded, though it was half a lie. Her body felt as if it were made of lead. "Yeah. Just tired."

"Close your eyes," he whispered. "Rest. I'll keep watch."

Her heart clenched at the caring protectiveness in his words. She wanted to resist, to insist on staying vigilant, independent, but the truth was she trusted him. More than she should. More than she'd ever thought she would.

Her head dipped against his shoulder. His arm shifted, wrapping around her, anchoring her.

"You really think we'll make it?" she asked, her voice barely above a whisper.

"I do," he whispered back. "Because we're in this together. And I won't let anything happen to you, Jayda. I'll get you home. I promise."

Home. Did she dare hope for such a thing? *God, I want to go home.*

Her eyes fluttered shut with the prayer on the tongue, and for the first time since the chaos began, she let herself rest.

Michael looked down at Jayda, at the delicate rise and fall of her chest. For once, her features weren't hardened with wit or sarcasm. She looked like her younger, more vulnerable self again. The girl he remembered being dropped off at his house. He felt guilt twist in his gut.

"Greta used to rest like that," Chuck said quietly, a smile tugging faintly at his mouth. "Right against my shoulder like she trusted me with the whole world."

Michael's throat tightened. "Your wife?"

Chuck nodded. "She was my whole life. Gone five years now, but it feels like yesterday." His eyes softened, going distant. "She trusted me more than I deserved."

Michael frowned. The words stung because they mirrored too closely his own truth. He let out a sharp exhale. "Jayda doesn't trust me. Not really. And she has every right not to. Right now, she's stuck with me. That's all."

Chuck chuckled, warm and low. "You know, I used to think Greta was stuck with me, too. But here's the thing—you never stop earning trust. Day by day, moment by moment. You keep showing up, no matter what."

Michael shook his head, bitterness rising. "You don't understand. I was awful to her. Back when she was a foster kid in my parents' house. I was older, selfish, too wrapped up in my own life to see what she needed. I treated her like she didn't belong." His voice dropped, rough with guilt. "She doesn't owe me anything now. Least of all trust."

Chuck's eyes flicked to him again, sharper this time. "Sounds to me like you're looking for penance."

Michael's jaw worked. "If I can help her now...if I can protect her, maybe I can make it right. Maybe I can wipe away some of the past."

Chuck studied him for a long moment. Then his voice softened again. "Is that all she is to you? A chance to fix your mistakes?"

Michael stiffened. He knew what Chuck was asking. He didn't want to admit it—not even to himself. "She's...more complicated than that."

"Complicated how?" Chuck pressed.

Michael's eyes slid to Jayda's sleeping face. The faintest smile tugged at her lips, as if she were dreaming something almost pleasant. His chest tightened. "She deserves more than I can give her. More than I have to give, and I deserve little."

Chuck's voice dropped low, as if he was letting him in on a secret. "Son, none of us deserves the good things. Not love, not forgiveness, not grace. But that's the whole point of Christmas. Hope for what we don't deserve. Hope for more than we could ever imagine. God's imagination far outstretches ours."

Michael stared at him, unsettled. "You're saying I should... what? Believe I get a do-over?"

"I'm saying you should ask God for what you want,"

Chuck said. "Not what you think you deserve. What do you want?"

Michael's throat tightened. He wanted to dodge the question, but it hung there, insistent. Finally, he whispered, "I want Jayda to be my friend."

Chuck's mouth quirked into a knowing smile. "And what if God wants to give you more than friendship?"

Michael's chest ached. He looked at her again, at how soft the lines of her face became in sleep. She was so pretty it hurt. His voice cracked with honesty. "That would far exceed what I'd dare ask for." He shook his head quickly, forcing the thought away. "But God's never been part of my life. Why would He give me anything?"

Chuck's answer came steadily. "Because He already has... because He's always been there for you whether you realized it or not. You just haven't opened your eyes to see it yet. To see Him and His secret gifts behind your back. But don't worry—I'll be praying He does."

The silence stretched after that, heavy but not uncomfortable. Michael leaned his head back against the seat, Jayda still resting against him, the warmth of her body grounding him more than he wanted to admit.

The rhythm of the tires against the road lulled the truck into a hushed cadence, the steady sound that could coax even the most restless mind toward quiet. Outside the passenger window, the world blurred in streaks of dark pine and snow-dusted fields, lit only by the occasional glow of farmhouse Christmas lights. Michael felt the weight of Jayda's head against his shoulder, her dark curls falling loose over his jacket, her breath soft and even.

Michael tilted his head slightly, careful not to jostle her. He shouldn't notice how warm she felt, or how her trust—even unconscious and unintentional—stirred a hope in him he had no right to claim. He shouldn't, but he did.

The car dipped slightly as they crossed a small bridge, headlights glancing off the frozen water below. Jayda stirred against him, murmuring something incoherent before settling again. Michael instinctively adjusted, comforting her, and when he glanced up, Chuck was smiling knowingly.

"You know," Chuck said, his eyes fixed on the dark stretch of highway ahead, "when Greta was alive, she used to tell me I had this annoying way of seeing through her excuses. She'd put on a brave face when she was hurting or scared, but I could always tell. Just like I could tell with your girl tonight. Fear's not something you can hide in the eyes." Chuck sent him a look that dared Michael to deny what he saw.

Michael swallowed, his jaw tightening. He nodded Chuck was right. Jayda was petrified, and so was he. Back at Chuck's house, Jayda had smiled, all polite and chipper, but her hands had trembled just enough to notice there was more. That fear wasn't imagined. It was real. And she had good reason.

Chuck continued, "The fear was right there, plain as day, in her eyes. That's why I jumped into action to take you. Whatever story you two gave me about meeting family...it isn't the whole truth, is it?"

Michael let out a long breath, barely above a whisper. "You're not wrong."

Chuck didn't respond right away, just kept his gaze on the road. Snowbanks blurred by, the highway empty except for the occasional pair of headlights slicing the dark.

Finally, Chuck spoke again. "You wanna tell me what's chasing her?"

Michael stared out the window, the snow falling at warp speed. He debated. He wasn't in the habit of spilling classified details to strangers. He always protected his sources for his articles, never sharing names.

At his hesitation, Chuck said, "Hm." Chuck leaned back

against the seat, a thoughtful sound rumbling in his chest. "You know, I used to be a cop."

Michael blinked, surprised. He studied the older man's weathered profile, the firm set of his mouth. "You?"

"Long time ago. Small-town force." Chuck's lips quirked with something that wasn't quite a smile. "You can trust me."

Former cop or not, Chuck was still a stranger. But he was neutral in all of this. Perhaps he could be of help as he had been all night. He'd opened his home, given them a getaway car, even if he didn't know it, and he asked no pertinent questions until this moment. And maybe Michael needed to get the truth off his chest.

"There are men after us," Michael said finally, his voice clipped.

Chuck's eyebrows ticked up. "After you—or her?"

"Her." He shifted, careful of Jayda's sleeping form. Michael exhaled slowly, careful not to wake Jayda. "She stumbled into this by accident. Wrong place, wrong time. But once they marked her, there was no going back. They want information. About a woman who witnessed a crime years ago. Something big. Guy went to prison. Jayda found something she wasn't supposed to. Now they think she knows where the witness is—or maybe even who she is."

Chuck gave a low whistle. "Sounds messy."

"That's one word for it."

"And this witness?" Chuck asked. "What's her deal? Testified? Flipped on someone? I had a few cases where people turned state's evidence. Sometimes they got deals. Sometimes they just wanted a clean conscience."

Michael's mouth twisted. "Who knows? We have a partial court case file and two pictures of her...and her name. Veronica Carlisle. Probably cut a deal for protection. Maybe witness protection. But if that's true, no one's confirming it.

Not the feds. The marshal we met in Chicago stonewalled us at every turn."

Chuck's eyes narrowed. "That's interesting, though I doubt the U.S. Marshals would share details with you anyway. But I'm sure you put them on alert. If she's in the program, she should be safe."

With no answers to the plaguing questions, they settled into silence for the rest of the trip, but it felt good for Michael to be honest with the man after all he had done for them that night.

Chuck pulled into the station, the crunch of his tires muffled by the falling snow. He shifted into park but didn't cut the engine. For a moment, the rumble filled the silence between them, until Chuck leaned an elbow on the wheel and spoke low.

"You know," he said, eyes on the windshield where flakes blurred the glass, "that woman you told me about, Veronica... maybe she didn't go into witness protection. Maybe she went on the run to protect herself."

Michael turned, curiosity piqued. "What do you mean?"

Chuck's mouth curved in a knowing, almost weary smile. "Some folks don't wait for the government to fix things. They run. Disappear. Start over under their own strength. If she did that, then what you need to figure out isn't where she went—it's who she was running from. Find that out, and you'll know who's chasing you, or I should say, Jayda now."

Michael sat with that thought heavy in his chest. It made sense. Veronica may not be just hiding but fleeing. Just like Jayda.

"It'll give you the upper hand," Chuck added. "If you can put the pieces together."

Michael opened his mouth, but movement beside him drew his attention. Jayda stirred, her head shifting slightly against his shoulder. Her eyes fluttered open, hazy with sleep, confusion flickering there before softening as she realized where she was.

"We're here?" she whispered.

"Yeah," Michael said gently. "We're here."

Chuck grinned, his weathered face warming at Jayda. "Glad you got some rest, young lady. You'll need it." He reached across the seat and squeezed her arm. "Stay safe, both of you." His gaze shifted back to Michael, more pointed now. "Take care of her. She's a precious gift."

Michael swallowed hard. He knew Chuck wasn't just talking about protection. The words hit him deep. *Precious gift.* He looked down at her again. She had trusted him enough to rest her head against him. And in that moment, he realized God had been giving him more than he ever imagined from the very start. Including Jayda.

And if he had missed that...what else had he missed?

"Now, get in there, and don't miss your train," Chuck ordered. "Or we'll be driving to the next stop in Denver."

Jayda jumped out into the storm with Michael right behind, waving to Chuck and running up the steps to the doors of the Kansas City, Missouri, station.

Jayda turned suddenly toward Michael. "Wait," she said, fumbling in her pocket. She pulled out the folded bills Simon had given them, tight in her fist. "I need to pay him back. He helped us—he deserves this."

Michael hesitated but nodded, watching as she darted back out to the parking lot. He followed a few steps behind, scanning the rows of snow-covered cars.

But the truck was gone. Not just gone—there weren't even tire tracks in the snow where he'd parked. Only smooth, untouched powder stretched across the lot. The fresh falling snow had already covered them.

Jayda stopped short, clutching the bills to her chest, her

expression caught between confusion and disbelief. "Michael...where did he go?"

Michael stared at the empty space, his breath frozen in his throat. He had no answer. He wrapped an arm around Jayda, doing as Chuck said, taking care of her.

"Come on, the train will be here soon. We can't miss it. Let's just thank God for Chuck tonight, okay?"

Jayda's stunned eyes watched him. "Yeah, let's thank God tonight. Did you know I asked Him to protect you? I think He just did."

Now Michael stood stunned. She had prayed for him, prayed for her enemy? Chuck had said Jayda was a precious gift, but being prayed for behind his back was the best gift anyone had ever given him.

Maybe Chuck was right, and God was always with him.

Ten

Jayda tugged her coat tighter around herself as she sat beside Michael on the old station's cracked bench. Her knee brushed his with every nervous shift, but he didn't seem to mind, and neither did she. A week ago, she wouldn't have depended on him for anything, and now she was leaning against his shoulder as though it was the most natural thing in the world.

What was going on between them? How was she trusting him so easily?

Trust. That was the word echoing through her skull like a mocking refrain. She had no business trusting him. Not after years of his torture, not after the way he had dismissed her when she'd been dropped off on his doorstep as if she chose this life. And yet here they were, side by side, waiting for the train with his family to arrive, both content in each other's presence.

Michael's voice broke the silence. "The train should be here soon."

"I can't believe we beat them."

"That we did." He chuckled, his smooth timbre poured out like hot caramel, but she heard the edge of relief in it too.

She turned, catching the glimmer of satisfaction in his eyes. Jayda offered a small smile. "Guess miracles happen."

The words felt almost foreign. She hadn't believed in miracles for a long time. But tonight, she let herself believe—just a little—that maybe the tide was turning. Maybe they weren't doomed after all.

The clock above the ticket counter ticked to five a.m., and at last the distant hum of an engine rumbled through the dark. The station windows rattled as the train pulled in, metal screeching against the frozen tracks.

They rose together, Michael's hand brushing against hers for just a second too long. The accidental touch made her pulse stumble. She glanced away quickly, hoping he hadn't noticed, and they made their way out onto the platform.

The doors hissed open. Silence. No chatter of early risers, no footsteps pounding down the corridor. They stepped inside and found the cars dimly lit for the overnight ride. Passengers were still tucked in their berths.

Michael released a quiet laugh. "Looks like nobody even realized we left."

A giddy ripple moved through Jayda's chest. "Do you think Simon told them?"

"Not likely. He would've let us handle it. And my mother would have called me relentlessly. He probably figured alerting everyone wasn't worth the panic."

"He was right," Jayda murmured. "And not just about that. I put you in danger, and I'm sorry."

"I wouldn't have done anything differently. Thank you for trusting me enough to ask for help."

They exchanged a look—half conspiratorial, half incredulous. A second chance. Somehow, impossibly, they'd been given one.

They drifted toward the dining car, which sat empty and still under the dim glow of the lamps. On one table lay the remnants of Ginny's late-night project with the twins—scissors, scraps of ribbon, twigs bundled together with string.

Michael picked up a twig, holding it between his fingers. "Mistletoe," he said, twisting it thoughtfully.

Jayda reached for a length of satin ribbon left behind, her fingers weaving through it absently. "She's got the kids making decorations? Does she ever turn the joy off?"

"Never." His tone carried amusement.

The quiet wrapped around them, but it wasn't heavy anymore. For the first time in days, Jayda felt almost...safe. Her gaze drifted to Michael's hands, steady and strong as he fiddled with the twig.

Then his words cut through the calm. "Chuck said something...while you were asleep. Could help us."

She looked up. "Tell me."

"We've been so worried about running, we haven't considered who exactly we're running from. If Veronica ran, who was she running from? It's probably the same person making the orders. Tell me about the case."

She shrugged. "I don't know much about it. Professor Dandridge said the case was in the news because the convict was getting out of jail this month. Albert Langston was the man in the case."

"Okay, so who was Veronica to Albert?" Michael withdrew his phone and searched for something.

"If she went into witness protection, we'll never know who she is now."

"What if she didn't?" He scrolled, eyeing her above the phone.

Jayda's grip on the ribbon tightened. "If she's not in witness protection, then she's on the run."

Michael's brows knit. "And that means?"

"It means she doesn't know she's being hunted—by them—and that we're in the way. Whichever of us reaches her first decides her fate."

He studied her face, his voice softening. "Why does this matter so much to you, Jayda? Besides your own safety?"

Her throat went dry. For a moment she considered brushing it off with a joke or a quick answer. But the weight of his striking eyes pressed against her defenses. But then hadn't they always? Hadn't those blues always read too much into her? She inhaled, steadying herself.

"Because I know what it feels like," she whispered.

He didn't speak. He waited.

Jayda set down the ribbon. Her voice trembled, but she forced herself forward. "I know what it's like to be forgotten. To be left out in the cold, trying to fend for yourself, wondering if anyone even remembers you exist. I lived on the streets. I lived in fear, not knowing who to trust. And no one was there to speak for me."

Michael's expression flickered with pain, but she pressed on.

"That's why I chose family law. There are kids out there—people—just like me, waiting for someone to fight for them. To be a voice for them. Veronica...she used her voice to put a monster behind bars. And now? She's on her own. And I can't let her stand alone."

The silence that followed was thick, charged with emotion. Michael reached for her hand, covering it with both of his. His touch was warm, grounding.

"I'm sorry," he whispered with a frown and remorse in his eyes. "I'm sorry I made you feel forgotten. If it takes the rest of my life, I'll make it up to you."

Jayda's chest ached, a mix of grief and longing colliding inside her. She pulled her hands back just slightly. "Michael... what are we doing? What's going on between us?"

His eyes softened, but his voice was steady. "Does it bother you? Us being close instead of fighting each other?"

She hesitated, searching his face. "Does it bother you?"

For a moment, neither spoke. Then Michael raised the twig mistletoe above their heads, a small smile tugging at his lips.

"This," he whispered, leaning closer, "feels right. Doesn't it feel right to you?"

Jayda's breath caught as his lips brushed against hers. The world tilted, her resistance crumbling with frightening ease.

"Yes," she murmured against his mouth. And then she deepened the kiss, her arms sliding around his neck, her fingers tangling through his hair.

The warmth, the safety, the hunger—it was dizzying.

And then—

A sharp gasp split the air.

Jayda's eyes flew open just as Michael pulled back, his expression stunned.

There, standing at the doorway of the dining car, was Ginny. Her hands clutched the twins close, the boys already giggling behind their palms, but Ginny's face was thunderous, her fury blazing even in the dim light.

The sliding door at the other end of the car opened at the same moment, and in walked the two men who had chased Jayda back in New Haven.

Looking from one end of the car to the other, from an irate Ginny to deadly mobsters, Jayda didn't know which was worse.

Michael stayed rooted to his spot, his body angled protectively toward Jayda. He had promised himself that he wouldn't let her get hurt again, but the two thick-shouldered men who stepped into the car didn't come for breakfast.

They were the men from Chicago. The fight in the alley. Most likely the men who shot out their tire and left them to freeze to death.

And now here to finish them, even with children in the car.

Jayda's gaze darted from Ginny to the men and back again. Before he could tell her to stay put, she bolted. The burst of speed sent her hair flying behind her like a banner. She darted toward the far door and up to Ginny.

"Jayda! How could you?" Ginny's voice cracked with anger and confusion.

"Not right now, Ginny. We have to get the kids out of here. Now!" Jayda picked up Timmy and took Tyler's hand, pulling him toward the exit.

"I want to talk to both of you. Michael, you're in big trouble, mister."

Michael kept his gaze on the men. "You're right about that, Mom. But we'll talk after. Go with Jayda. Now." His tone held authority, and thankfully his mother listened.

Michael squared his shoulders and readied for a fight. In no way was he letting the men past him. His blood thundered in his ears, adrenaline building.

"Well," he said, his voice rough, "we meet again."

The man on the left sneered, his jaw lined with old, pockmarked scars. "Get out of the way, Blair."

"We don't want you," the other added. "We just want what the girl has."

Michael flexed his jaw. "And what's that?"

The scarred man's eyes narrowed. "The pictures. After that, we'll leave her alone."

"I don't believe you. Who is Veronica Carlisle?"

The second man grunted. "Veronica. She was mine. My

wife. The broad turned on me. Called the cops on a job I was doing and got my boss sent to prison. She needs to pay. She thought she could run with our secrets." His lips curled in a snarl. "But wives don't betray their husbands. She betrayed family. Now she'll pay for it. And anyone who protects her—" He leaned forward, menace dripping from every syllable. "—pays too."

Michael clenched his fists. Every instinct screamed at him to lunge, to fight, but he forced his tone cool, almost mocking. "So let me get this straight. You married a woman smarter than you, who turned you in, who escaped you, and you think the best revenge is chasing down a law student because she picked up the wrong envelope?"

The scarred man's nostrils flared. "Move, Blair. Now."

Instead, Michael stepped sideways—just enough to angle them closer to the vestibule doors. His eyes flicked toward the glass reflection, catching movement down the hall. Timing. He needed only timing.

"You know what's funny?" Michael said, tilting his head like he wasn't trembling inside. "You could have learned something from Veronica."

"What's that?"

"How to run."

Before they could ask what he meant, Michael yanked the emergency brake handle by the wall. The train lurched hard. Both men stumbled, their balance thrown, and Michael shoved them back with a grunt, slamming one against the steel wall.

The far door slid open. Two more men entered, guns drawn. For a breathless second, Michael thought reinforcements for the mob had arrived—until the words rang out:

"U.S. Marshals! Hands where we can see 'em!"

Relief surged so hard it left Michael dizzy.

The two Chicago men froze. Michael shoved the scarred

one again, tipping him toward the marshals, who moved swiftly, handcuffs snapping in seconds. The second man spat curses, thrashing, but Michael helped pin him until the cuffs bit home.

"Good work," one marshal grunted to Michael, hauling the mobster upright.

Michael's chest heaved as the men were dragged away. "Don't thank me yet. Jayda ran. I have to find her."

The marshals exchanged a look. "She'll be safe now with these two off your tail. Go."

Michael didn't need more permission. He bolted down the aisle, shoving the next sliding door aside until he reached her cabin.

Inside, Jayda sat on the bunk, Ginny beside her, one hand wrapped tight around Jayda's trembling fingers. The twins weren't there.

Michael froze. "Where are the kids?"

"With Ed in the next car," Ginny said quickly. Then she patted the bed. "Sit. We're going to talk."

Michael blinked. Talk? Now? He'd just fought mobsters, nearly lost Jayda, and Ginny wanted to *chitchat*?

But his mother's eyes flashed with that familiar maternal command, and Michael obeyed, sinking to the bunk across from them.

Ginny folded her arms. "I don't know what game you two are playing, but enough. Jayda, you've rejected us over and over, but I just found you kissing my son. So, which is it? What game are you playing here?"

Jayda's face flushed crimson. Her lips parted to answer, but Michael cut in, leaning forward. "It was my fault. I pushed it. Don't blame her."

But Jayda shook her head. "No. Michael, stop. She's right." She turned to Ginny, voice breaking. "I owe you the truth. I'm sorry. For all the ways I turned my back on your love. I always felt guilty for letting myself forget my birth mother, like it was a betrayal to let you take her place."

Ginny's face softened instantly. She clasped Jayda's hand tighter. "Oh, sweetheart. I never wanted to take her place. I wanted only to give you a home. A place where you were loved."

Tears filled Jayda's eyes, spilling down her flushed cheeks.

Ginny looked at Michael then, her eyes sharper than any knife. "But my son. He did everything he could to push you away. So tell me, Michael—what's changed?"

Michael's throat closed. He tried to look away, but Ginny's stare demanded truth.

"Nothing," he said finally, voice raw. "Nothing's changed. I wanted Jayda to have a place she could be loved. Except...I think I always loved her in a different way. One that you wouldn't have been happy about."

Ginny and Jayda both went still.

Michael turned fully to Jayda, his heart racing, but before he could make sense of his words, a scream shattered the air.

"Help! Someone help me!"

They all bolted upright.

Caroline's voice ripped down the hall, frantic and raw. "My baby—oh, God, Simon's dead! He's dead!"

Michael flew out of the cabin, Jayda and Ginny on his heels. They shoved into Simon's room to find Caroline crouched over the bed, her hands shaking over his still body.

Simon lay sprawled with a single bullet hole in his forehead.

Michael staggered back. "No..."

"Someone shot him!" Caroline shrieked.

Michael whirled. "Stay here—I'll get the marshals!"

He sprinted down the train cars, noticing the snow still coming down in the middle of nowhere, the sun rising from the east. The train had stopped, but a conductor could not be found. When he reached the end, it was also empty but a few passengers roaming about wondering why the train had stopped.

No marshals were there to help. If they left with their two prisoners, they left them with a killer on board.

Eleven

Simon hadn't been her friend, not really. But he had been an ally. He was a man who carried a burden of secrets he never explained, a man who piqued their curiosities with intriguing, brilliant stories that could have been as fake as his smiles, but now she would never know. Now he was nothing but a body cooling fast in the isolated mountains—and all for a silly train ride reunion.

All because of her.

Jayda's throat tightened, standing over his bunk, wanting to cover him up. He deserved more than this.

She whispered, "I'm sorry. I tried to keep you out of this mess." She didn't understand why he had been killed. He knew nothing. Had the assassin made a terrible mistake?

Or was there something she had missed?

She wanted off this train. Outside, snow blurred the window, but they were stopped in the mountains in the middle of nowhere. Inside, silence pressed like another death. No one was safe, on or off.

The door rattled. Jayda jumped to her feet, wiping her hands on her coat just as the knob turned. The conductor filled the doorway, his cap dusted white, showing he had been outside. His face paled as he took in Simon sprawled across the bunk.

"My God. So it's true," he whispered. "What happened here?"

Jayda fought to keep her voice calm. "He was shot. There's a killer on board." She swallowed hard, praying the conductor couldn't hear the quiver in her words. "You need to call the police."

He stared at Simon and then warily at Jayda. "We'll have to radio ahead. You should go back to your cabin, Miss. Everyone will need to be accounted for...the police will need to speak to you."

Jayda nodded, gripping her coat closed. "His parents are in the next car, in Ginny's cabin, number 25, I think, if you need them. That's where they are."

Her heart hammered so hard she thought he must hear it echoing off the walls. She must look and sound guilty, and maybe she was, even if she didn't pull the trigger.

As the conductor ushered her from the room, she spotted Simon's phone behind the open door. Her pulse jumped. If Simon had been sending messages, if he had been playing some dangerous game, then the answers might be right there.

She followed the conductor out and returned to her room.

"Go on," he said firmly. "The authorities will take it from here."

Jayda nodded but waited until she heard him rush out of the car and into the next before she stepped back into the corridor. In her wallet was Simon's extra keycard from the day he had slipped it to her, though she never planned to use it. He had just been suave Simon being Simon, having no idea she was in trouble.

Or had he?

Jayda needed to find out. She removed the card from her

wallet, never thinking she'd need it to break into his room because he was dead.

His door lock clicked over, and she rushed into the room. Quickly, she bent and reached behind the door, slipping the phone into her pocket with one smooth movement and backed out in seconds.

Her breath caught when she heard the train car door slide open. She leaned against the wall, her fingers clutching the stolen phone as if it were a live grenade. Two men talked about the police being called and about checking every room while Jayda slunk back to her cabin and slipped inside. The train began to move again, almost knocking her over.

"The Denver police will take it from there," one man said as they passed her room.

With the door locked and the shades drawn, her hands shook as she swiped the screen, remembering when Simon had input his code at breakfast one morning. She opened his texts —one thread caught her eye—short, sharp exchanges with someone saved only as "A."

A: *Don't lose them.*

Simon: *They trust me.*

A: *Trust is temporary. Deliver the girl. Now.*

Her stomach dropped.

Deliver the girl?

Simon: *I want out.*

A: *Too late. You've already been paid.*

Jayda pressed her palm over her mouth to keep from crying out. That girl was her. Simon hadn't been protecting her—he'd been playing a dangerous and traitorous game. Maybe he regretted it in the end, and that's why they killed him? Or maybe he didn't know who he was messing with, but the truth stared right at her. All his ploys and flirtations had been calculated. His reason for being on this train had nothing to do with family.

Her hands trembled as she scrolled down, sinking her heart further, cutting her deeper.

S: *Train stop in Chicago. Second payment ready IF you deliver her to me. Otherwise...*

The betrayal was complete, the weight of it crushing. Simon's kindness, his cryptic help—it had all been part of a bargain. Maybe he'd turned at the last second. Maybe that's why he was dead. But it didn't matter now.

She shoved the phone into her coat pocket and sat heavily on the bunk. For a moment, fear suffocated her. If Simon had been ready to hand her over, then who was waiting to collect? The hitman? Was he on this train now? How many men were on this train, hunting her down, waiting for the moment she showed herself? All for the documents they thought would lead them to Veronica but wouldn't.

Unless...maybe they would, and she was missing the clues.

She huffed at taking the marshal's word for it. He'd let her think they wouldn't lead anywhere, possibly for his own gain.

The storm outside grew louder while the one within her reared up in anger. Snow slashed against the windows as she wasted no time, slipping the envelope of documents into her coat and out into the corridor.

The train swayed, a beast roaring through the storm, racing to the authorities.

Jayda moved quickly down the narrow passage, then pushed out onto the metal grating between cars.

The cold hit like a hammer. Wind screamed in her ears, icy needles slicing her cheeks. She gripped the railing, leaning forward, her breath torn away before she could exhale. The snow blurred everything into a blinding white void.

She pulled the envelope from her coat, fingers stiff. The papers inside—names, dates, numbers—felt like poison. If she tossed them now, let the storm swallow them, maybe this nightmare would die with Simon.

But then she saw it—the backside of one photograph. On the back, scrawled in faint pen was *Lombard Street.*

Her breath caught. Lombard Street. San Francisco. Was that where she went?

Jayda held the photo tight, clutching it close. Not ready to let it go. There might be more she missed.

Turning to the next car, movement behind her spun her back around just as a figure lunged from the adjoining car. A man—broad-shouldered, face half-hidden under a hood. His hand shot out, gripping her arm, slamming her into the metal wall. Pain burst in her shoulder. The envelope tumbled, and before she could stop it, the papers scattered into the storm.

"No!" she screamed, scrambling after them. But the man yanked her back, his fist raised.

She ducked, the punch banging off her temple. Stars exploded in her vision. She kicked hard, her boot connecting with his shin. He snarled, shoving her against the railing. The metal bit into her spine, cold and painful. Icy snow whipped at her face, stinging like tiny knives all over.

Fear surged. She was seconds from being thrown, from vanishing into the white abyss, over jagged rocks and sprawling gorges. The sound of the train roared in her ears, louder than her own scream.

But beneath the terror, something fierce burned. She wasn't just a girl from the New Haven streets, fighting to survive. She was fighting to live. She had a purpose and things to do. She had...Michael. Whatever was happening between them, she needed to explore it. He'd told his mother he'd always loved her.

Was that what this was between them, always lying beneath their quarrels?

Was it love?

The man lunged again, grabbing for her throat. She twisted, using his momentum to slam his arm against the rail.

He grunted, stumbling, but he was still stronger, heavier. He shoved back, forcing her onto the narrow edge of the platform. Her boots slipped on ice. Nothing between her and the drop but a few inches of frozen steel.

I'm going to die. I'll never tell Michael I—

"Jayda!"

The shout ripped through the wind. Michael burst from the adjoining car, eyes wild. He grabbed the man from behind, wrenching him away from her. The force sent them both crashing into the wall.

Jayda collapsed to her knees, clutching the rail, breath ragged.

The fight blurred—fists slamming, grunts, the squeak of boots on metal. Michael fought like a man possessed, every strike carrying a desperation she'd never seen before. He wasn't just protecting her. He was fighting to finish this chase once and for all.

"No, Michael," Jayda shouted to get his attention. She couldn't let him kill the man. He was better than that.

The attacker pulled back and hit Michael, sending him flying back, landing half off the train.

Jayda dropped to the grate to hold on to him, but the man straddled Michael, choking him. Jayda had to let go, praying he wouldn't fall off the edge. If only she had her stun gun. But she didn't, and all she could rely on was her own strength. Lifting her leg, she kicked the man in the back of the head, using the heel of her boot repeatedly to get him to let go. When the man turned to face her, reaching for leg, Michael grabbed the man and lifted him over his head and out into the swirling snow.

But the momentum sent Michael slipping further over the edge.

Jayda screamed and reached for his shirt before she lost him forever. She landed on him, locking her boot on the railing, holding him with all her might, stopping him from following the man over.

With their faces inches apart, she shouted, "Hold on!" She gripped his coat while ice whipped at their faces. "Don't you dare go over!"

His blue eyes locked on her. But she didn't see fear for himself. She saw concern for her. "Are you hurt? Did he hurt you?"

"Don't worry about me. Just stay on this train! I mean it, Michael! Don't you dare leave me alone!"

Visible strength filled his eyes. He growled as he used every muscle in his body to lift himself up against the momentum of the train's pace, and soon they were sitting side by side, their breaths heaving from exertion.

Jayda shook her head, tears blurring her vision. "I thought —" Her voice cracked. "I thought you were gone."

He lifted a weak arm, pulling her against him, his coat rough, his arms fierce. She buried her face against his chest, the beat of his heart loud and steady beneath her cheek. For the first time since this nightmare began, she let herself believe they were safe. Just for this moment. She knew there would be more.

But for now, it was just them.

The train thundered on into the Rockies, but for Jayda, the storm inside finally broke, and she knew she needed Michael beside her. Not just right now but forever. Not just to survive this train ride but to survive *everything*.

And that realization terrified her more than the fight.

Michael's hand lingered on her cheek, thumb brushing away snow. His eyes softened, but his jaw stayed tight. "We're not safe yet. There could still be others wandering about on this train. But as long as I'm here, you're not alone."

Jayda swallowed hard. For the first time in years, she believed it.

Michael kept his arm snug around Jayda's shoulders as they crept down the narrow corridor of their sleeper car. Every step he took was calculated, his body angled just enough to shield her from the curious eyes of fellow passengers who peeked out of their cabins in fear. Simon's body had only been discovered an hour ago, and the atmosphere aboard the train stretched thin with tension. Every noise caused people to jump.

Jayda leaned slightly against him, her stride slower than normal. She was still shaken, weak from saving him. Michael held her tight for her reassurance but also for his own. The tremor in her hand when she smoothed her hair back behind her ear made him want to tell her it was over, that she could breathe again, but he knew better. These men weren't going anywhere.

Michael reached his cabin. He fished out the key, slid it into the lock, and pushed the door open, expecting solitude to regroup.

Only they weren't alone.

His parents sat waiting for him.

"We need to talk," his mother said from the corner, her voice taut with maternal command. She sat rigidly on the bench, her hands folded in her lap like a judge ready to hand down a sentence. Beside her, Ed leaned back, arms crossed, his brow creased in the grim frown Michael knew too well.

For a heartbeat, Michael froze. His hand tightened instinctively on Jayda's arm.

"Sure but can you give us a few moments?" he asked, masking the jolt of alarm with forced calm. "Everyone's on edge."

Ginny's eyes swept immediately to Jayda. A flicker of calculation passed across her features, her disapproval barely veiled. "We have a lot that needs to be discussed. Privately."

Jayda shifted uncomfortably. "I can give you time—"

"No." Michael's voice came out sharper than he intended. He tightened his hold on her hand before she could retreat. "She stays."

"Michael," his dad rumbled, his deep baritone cutting through the cramped air of the cabin. "The conductor already announced that everyone is to return to their rooms until we reach Denver. You shouldn't even be wandering through the cars. And yet here you are...with Jayda."

The last word was weighted, as if Jayda was an interloper —someone who didn't belong.

Michael bristled. "It's *Jayda*," he snapped. "Your..." *Daughter?* That didn't feel right. "Family," he said instead. "I'm not leaving her alone. Not when there's a killer on this train."

Ginny leaned forward slightly, her gaze fixed, deliberate. "We're not blind, Michael. We see what's happening between you two. But this...this sudden attachment concerns us."

Jayda looked down at the floor. He could feel her wanting to disappear into the narrow space between the bunks.

Michael angled himself, shielding her as best he could in the cramped space. "It's not sudden," he said evenly, though anger boiled beneath the surface. "It's been there for years. Since high school, if you want the truth."

Ed blinked, surprised. "High school? Michael, you've never said—"

"Of course I said nothing," he cut his father off. His voice rose, and he forced himself to rein it back, lowering the volume but not the intensity. "I said nothing because I knew what you'd think. That it was wrong. So I hurt her instead. I pushed my feelings down and made her time in our home miserable, all to avoid the truth. I won't hurt her anymore, and I won't deny how I feel either. If that bothers you, so be it. I won't be apologizing either."

Jayda's head jerked up at that. He felt her eyes on him, wide and startled. But he couldn't stop. The dam had cracked, and years of unspoken words rushed forward.

Ginny pressed her hand to her chest. "Michael. She was like a sister to you."

"No." His denial was fierce, final. "She was never a sister. She was the girl who challenged me to think of someone else other than myself, and I failed her. But never again. And I won't lie to myself...or you. I won't lie about how I feel about her."

His words fell into the cabin with the weight of revelation.

Silence stretched. Ginny's lips parted, then closed again. Ed's arms dropped from their folded stance, his brows furrowing deeper, conflicted.

"And how is that?" Ed asked.

"Simple. I love her."

Jayda exhaled on a rush behind him, as if the very air had been knocked from her lungs. He turned, and she took a step back, shaking her head slowly.

"Michael..." Her voice trembled. "Don't do this right now. It's not a good time."

"Do what? Fight for you? Like you just put your life at risk to fight for me?" he asked, desperation creeping in now because he could feel her slipping away, retreating. "Let me tell the truth. To finally admit what I've denied for years."

She backed toward the door. "Not like this. Not now. Simon's dead. You need your family right now."

But he followed, words tumbling too fast to stop. "*You* are family. I want you in my life, Jayda. I want you to be part of the Blairs. Always. But by marriage."

The last two words cracked the air.

Ginny gasped, covering her mouth with her hand. Ed muttered in disbelief under his breath.

Jayda froze at the door, her hand hovering on the knob.

For a second, she met his gaze, her eyes full of panic. Then she shook her head. "I can't—" Her voice broke. "I can't do this."

She pulled open the door and slipped out into the corridor.

"Jayda." Michael lunged after her. His parents called his name, but he didn't care. He chased her down the narrow hall, the train rocking beneath his feet. "Wait. Please just wait."

But Jayda didn't slow. She reached her cabin, nearly colliding with the conductor, who stepped out of her room at the same time.

"Miss," the conductor said firmly, raising a hand, holding a phone in it—a phone that looked like Simon's. "You need to return to your room immediately. Orders from the police. We'll be arriving at Denver station shortly, and they've requested to speak with you first. You're not to go anywhere."

The train slowed. Jayda looked back at Michael, resolve written on her face. She was a suspect?

"Go back to your family," Jayda said to him and entered her room, the latch of her door saying what she didn't.

She would handle this like everything else in her life.

Alone.

[illegible]

She pulled open the door and slipped out into the corridor.

[illegible]

[illegible]

"Miss," the conductor said, [illegible]

[illegible]

[illegible]

[illegible]

She wound her hand [illegible]

Alone.

Twelve

The train groaned as it pulled into Denver, metal wheels screeching against the rails like fingernails on glass. Jayda sat rigidly on the bench in her cabin, hands clasped in her lap so tightly her knuckles had gone white. She couldn't look out the window, couldn't bear the way the city seemed to rush past as if the world itself was moving faster than she could think. She would be questioned about Simon's murder, and yet, all she could hear in her head was Michael's confession of love.

Of marriage.

The conductor's voice cut over the loudspeaker, steady but grim. "We are arriving at Denver Station. Passengers, remain in your assigned cabins until police escort you for questioning."

Marriage?

She couldn't process the idea. Michael Blair *loved* her and wanted to *marry* her. Was this one of his tricks? Maybe he hit his head when he nearly fell off the train. The man was infuriating. One moment he hated her, and the next he wanted her to be part of the Blair family by *marriage?* Not by childhood circumstance, not by obligation, but by forever vows?

Her heart thudded against her ribs. She had denied his words and bolted. If she let herself believe them—believe in him—what then? What if she said yes to him only to be snatched by the mob next week? What if she ruined him just by existing in his life?

The train jolted to a stop, knocking her thoughts out of orbit.

And true to the conductor's word, a knock came on her door. Her escort had arrived.

The exterior doors hissed open for her walk of shame. Denver greeted her with the bite of icy mountain air and the flashing red-and-blue lights of waiting police cruisers. Officers in dark jackets lined the platform, their breath fogging in the night air.

"Miss Simone?"

Jayda looked up, blinking, as an officer with tired eyes and a notepad stopped in front of her. His tone was polite, but there was no mistaking the edge of suspicion beneath it.

"Yes," she said, voice steady despite the gallop of her heart.

"Please come with us for questioning."

Suddenly Michael stood behind her, and Jayda nearly leaned into him. He must have been watching for her out of his cabin window.

"I'm going with her," he said.

"No," Jayda replied, looking at the officer. "It's fine. I can handle this. I don't need...him."

She didn't mean to make her words sound cruel, but she didn't look back either as she continued her walk to the interrogation.

The small room inside the station that became the questioning room was small but functional, painted a weary gray that looked like it hadn't been refreshed in twenty years. A metal table separated her from two detectives—Detective Hollins, who did most of the talking, and Detective Fields, who scribbled notes in quick, impatient bursts.

Hollins leaned forward, folding his hands. "Miss Simone, you took a phone from the murder scene of Simon Blair. Can you walk us through why that happened?"

Jayda drew a slow breath. She'd practiced this in her head, wishing she'd majored in criminal law, but knew enough from her one semester to keep it simple and true.

Or ask for counsel.

"Simon was a friend," she said. "Or so I thought. He was trying to help me, but I wouldn't let him. Now, I know it's good that I hadn't trusted him."

"Help you with what?"

Jayda bit her lip, knowing how this would sound. "The mob's been trying to kill me. I'm on a hit-list of some kind."

Hollins' eyebrows arched. "Is that so? And how did you manage that?"

Jayda had no choice but to tell the truth. "I tasered one of them. He was stealing a file from the library. He had a gun. I only protected myself."

"There was a man from the mob at the library?" Hollins' eyes squinted.

Jayda winced. "I know that sounds absurd, but it's true. He was looking for the whereabouts of a woman who turned state's evidence on someone. She's also on the hit list. The file had information about where she went."

"And where's that?"

Jayda shook her head. "I don't feel comfortable sharing that information. And it has nothing to do with why Simon is dead."

Hollins smirked. "Fine. Where's the file now?"

"Gone."

"Gone? How?"

"It blew off the train when a man was trying to kill me."

Hollins chuckled. "Convenient. But I guess that's a better excuse than your dog ate it."

Jayda pursed her lips in annoyance. "Make fun of me all you want. But it's all true. And the longer you talk to me, the faster Simon's killer gets away. If he survived the fall from the train, that is."

Fields' pen scratched against the paper. Hollins tilted his head. "Okay, we'll circle back to that one. First, let's back up to the question of why Simon is dead. You say he was working in organized crime."

"*With*. He was paid to deliver me to the mob."

"That's a big assumption."

"Not an assumption. It's all on his phone. I'm assuming the conductor gave it to you? The passcode is 3341. Read it for yourselves."

"We will."

Jayda forced herself to meet his eyes. "He pretended to be my friend, and I think maybe he was at the end. He gave me the cash they gave them. I believe he had been paid to kidnap me. He might have felt guilty and told them he would not fulfill their deal, and that's why they killed him."

"What made you touch evidence at a crime scene?" Ramirez asked suddenly. "I'm told you're studying to be a lawyer. Did they not teach you about evidence?"

Her pulse skipped. "Of course. But when your life is on the line, legalities become blurred."

The door burst open, with Ed standing behind it. "Jayda, don't say another word. Detectives, we're done here until I have talked with my client. Let's go, Jayda."

Fields looked up from his pad. "Thank you for your information, Miss Simone."

Ramirez studied her like a puzzle with too many missing pieces. But after a long silence, he sat back. "You're free to go for now. Don't leave town until we say you're free to leave."

Relief and fear tangled inside her chest. She stood too quickly, her chair scraping against the floor. Racing to Ed, he wrapped an arm around her and closed the door on the men.

"Next time, ask for help. I had no idea they were considering you as a suspect. If it hadn't been for Michael coming to tell me, you would still be in there incriminating yourself."

"I just told them the truth."

"Oh, sweetheart, truth and justice don't always go together in this world. Learn that now."

Michael stood waiting outside the room, pacing like a tethered animal. The second he saw her, he was at her side, hands gripping her shoulders.

"What did they say? What did you tell them? I want the details."

"They let me go," she said, her voice harsher than she intended. This was the new Michael, not the one she fought with every breath. He'd said he cared...that he loved her.

"That's not what I asked."

She shook her head, unwilling to share the news about his cousin. "Michael, this isn't one of your stories. There's no angle you can wrap up in two thousand words. It's complicated, and I don't think you'll want to know the truth. It'll come out, and it's going to be ugly."

His jaw tightened. "You're wrong. I see at least three stories here, and they don't end well for you. They're saying you tampered with evidence at the crime scene. What happened?"

"Stop." The word came out sharp, but she couldn't let him keep peeling this out of her. Simon was his family, not hers, regardless of his confession of love and marriage. Simon was a blood relative of his. She was nothing. "This isn't a headline. This is my life. I did what I had to do. That's all."

Michael leaned close, whispering, "Tell me. I can handle it."

Jayda looked at Ed, not wanting to hurt either of these men. But she knew the truth would come out and crush them anyway.

Before Michael could push further, the rest of the Blair family appeared down the hall—Ginny with a distraught Caroline and Henry trailing behind, the twins in their hands.

Simon's parents would be devastated to learn what he had done. Jayda didn't want to be the one to tell them.

Ginny stepped forward, wrapping Jayda in a motherly embrace that caught her off guard. "Are you all right?"

"I'm fine," Jayda said, though her voice trembled against Ginny's shoulder.

"Are you in trouble? Ed will help you. But you need to tell us what's going on."

Jayda lifted her head to face Caroline and Henry. "It's about Simon. He did something...terrible. It's what got him killed."

Heavy sadness swept over Caroline's face, but the woman nodded once as if she knew someday this would happen. "Be honest with us, Jayda. What did my boy do this time?"

Detective Hollins stepped out of the room with Simon's phone. "Your story checks out, Miss Simone. I still want you to hang around for a while. I have some other questions about the men chasing you. We find them, and we find Simon's killer."

Caroline let out a cry. "What did he do to get himself killed?"

Hollins replied, "Simon took a bribe to deliver Miss Simone to the killer. When he didn't, he got himself killed."

Michael searched Jayda's face, his eyes darkened with shock and fear that made her chest ache.

"I'm sorry," she said to him and then to them all. "But it's true. Simon and was willing to put my life at risk for money. I took his phone from his cabin to read his texts. They confirmed it. So yes, I tampered with evidence, but I had to know the truth. I had to know if he had died because of me. I was just as shocked and hurt by what I read. But he gave me the money. I believe Simon regretted what he had done. But there was no going back for him."

Caroline turned, embracing her husband, the two needing this time together.

Jayda stepped back from the Blair family, needing to separate. "I'm going to go on to find Veronica. I know where she is. She needs to be warned. But I'll handle this from here on my own. I'm so sorry to you all."

"No," Ginny said firmly, pulling back. "We've decided something. All of us."

Jayda frowned. "What?"

"We're not going home."

Jayda blinked. "What do you mean? The train's going west. You can get a flight from Denver and be back in Connecticut tomorrow."

Ginny shook her head, her chin lifted with stubborn resolve. "Michael told us about protecting Veronica. If you need to keep going, then we're going too. You're not doing this alone."

Jayda's throat tightened. "No. This isn't your fight. It's unnecessary."

Ed crossed his arms, his broad frame blocking any chance of argument. "Family doesn't walk away from each other. Ever."

"Exactly," Ginny said, her voice thick with emotion. "We've been fighting for you since the day you stepped into our home. And we will never stop. Do you understand? Never."

Jayda swallowed hard. She wanted to argue, to tell them

they didn't understand what they were walking into, but the lump in her throat choked off the words.

Michael's voice cut through, quiet but firm. "Now I see four stories. And this one—this one's the winner."

Jayda's eyes flicked to him, startled. He wasn't talking about journalism anymore. She could hear it in his voice. He was talking about her. About them. About family, about belonging, about love.

And she didn't know whether to run or to stay.

The Denver train station buzzed with life, but Michael sat still and quiet on the long benches with his family, their group huddled together waiting to be questioned further. The whistle of their train to the west rang out as it pulled away from the station without them.

Michael's notebook weighed heavy in his jacket pocket. His journalist brain throbbed with unwritten sentences, paragraphs that clawed to get out. A mob entanglement on a train. A foster daughter running from danger. A murder in the snowbound Rockies. He'd never stumbled across a story this wild but also painfully personal. He had enough material for at least three exposés, maybe even a book.

But the thought of putting Jayda's face in print—her name, her life—made his gut twist. For once, Michael Blair wasn't sure he wanted the story at all.

Harold would surely fire him if he didn't produce by Christmas Eve in five days' time.

Aunt Caroline and Uncle Henry sat across from him, their grief unspoken but blatant. Caroline's hands were folded tight in her lap, white-knuckled, holding herself together by sheer will. Henry, normally a man of steady calm, seemed hollowed out, his gaze on the floor but full of disappointment. His arms draped around the twins, who seemed to sense the heaviness around them and sat still.

Henry and Caroline had lost Simon, their son, their flesh and blood. But it wasn't just grief that filled their eyes—it was fury. They wanted the men who had used Simon, bought his loyalty, pushed him into betrayal. They wanted justice for their son. Michael could see it in every tense line of Henry's jaw.

Beside him, Ginny and Ed flanked Jayda like guards. Ginny had an arm wrapped over Jayda's shoulder, as though holding onto her made her part of the family she'd longed for since Jayda was fourteen. Ed sat quietly, a reliable presence, his eyes flicking toward every uniform that passed by, ready to protect.

Michael leaned forward, elbows on his knees, eyes on Jayda. She hadn't spoken since Ginny announced they would continue to help her. Her chin rested in her palm, her dark eyes far away, locked on something only she could see.

She was thinking of San Francisco. He knew it. She'd tried to convince the detectives that she had to get there, that it was imperative, life or death. But they'd told her in clipped voices not to leave Denver. "You're material witnesses," they'd said. "Stay put."

Now they were stranded, watching their ride vanish down the rails.

Michael needed to talk to Jayda alone. To break through the wall that she'd erected between them after he'd admitted his feelings for her.

Michael swallowed hard, made up his mind, then rose and touched Jayda's elbow. "Walk with me a second?"

She glanced at him, then reluctantly nodded. They stepped away from the cluster, the station noise filling in the silence between them. He led her near the wall, beneath a flickering departure board.

"Why are you pushing me away?" he asked low. "What have I done to cause this? I know I hurt you for years, but I really want to spend the rest of my life making it up to you. Please let me try."

She crossed her arms, defensive. "I'm running for my life. I'm running to protect Veronica's. That's all I can focus on right now, Michael."

Michael stopped short of trying to convince her to let him in. "Fine," he muttered. "But don't expect me to stop worrying. Or following you into whatever mess is next. You focus on running, and I'll just keep up with you. Deal?"

Her expression softened, just slightly. Then, a smile twitched on her lips. She looked up at him through her eyelashes. "Fine. For now. But only because you're kind of growing on me."

Michael flashed a grin. "Like a boil or a smile?"

"Strangely, both." She turned away. "I need some water."

"I'll go with you."

She waved him off. "You're being ridiculous. There are police everywhere. I'll be fine. Stay here."

Michael ground his teeth but did as she asked. With law enforcement swarming the place, he wasn't too worried, as long as she was within view.

She walked toward the drinking fountain against the far wall and pressed the lever. Nothing. She frowned, glanced over her shoulder at him. Their eyes locked.

Then, she stepped around the corner and disappeared down the hall.

Michael took a step but paused, not wanting to upset her with even more smothering. But the seconds stretched too long. His heart lurched, and he crossed the floor of the station.

When he reached the corner, she was gone.

Thirteen

Jayda struggled against the leather glove over her mouth and the vice grip that held her arms so tight she couldn't fill her lungs. Stars flashed before her eyes, but somewhere off in the distance she could hear Michael calling for her. She whimpered, wanting to call out to him for help, now that she couldn't any longer.

As soon as she was carried out a side door, a black car waited for them.

It happened so fast her brain could hardly stitch the images together of the gleam of tinted glass before her and three men in dark coats moving as one. Their footsteps pounded the pavement, tossing her inside the vehicle. Before she could scream, she heard Michael shouting.

"Let her go!"

And then he was beside her, thrown to the floor.

"No!" Jayda cried, twisting against the wall of muscle that was the man who still held her.

The door slammed shut with a heavy, last sound of captivity, and the car lurched forward. Jayda strained toward the door, heart hammering. The train station blurred past—and in that quick streak of motion, she saw them.

Ginny. Ed. Caroline. Henry. The twins.

They were running after the car, faces tight with fear, with hands waving, voices shouting—though Jayda could barely hear through the sealed glass. They were no match for the accelerating vehicle. Within seconds, they slowed, the defeat in their postures breaking Jayda's heart.

Then, just before the car turned the corner, Ginny pressed two fingers to her lips and whistled a sharp, commanding sound that carried even through the glass. Jayda's eyes widened as a yellow cab swerved into view. Ginny pointed, yelling instructions as she and Ed jumped in the back, leaving the twins with Caroline and Henry. The cab raced away from the curb, closing the gap between them.

Tears filled Jayda's eyes at the sight, conflicted about the danger everyone was in because of her but never feeling so loved.

The crisp, unmistakable metallic click of a gun being loaded twisted Jayda back around. Her breath stilled at the sight, drying her eyes in an instant.

It was "Scar" who sat across from her. The same man from the law library. The man she'd tasered. His dark suit looked perfectly pressed, his hair slicked back, and the pistol in his hand pointed right at her would do more than her stun gun ever did to him.

"My turn," he said, his voice a gravel chuckle.

Michael shifted instantly, sliding in front of her like a shield. "You want her, you go through me."

Jayda's throat constricted. "Michael, don't." She reached for him, her palm flat against his chest, meaning to push him back, meaning to protect him instead.

But then, from the other side, another man swung the

butt of a pistol. The crack against Michael's skull was sickening. His body folded to the floor before Jayda could shout, no.

"Michael!" Her scream tore out of her as she dropped beside him. His chest still rose and fell, but his eyes were closed, lashes dark against his cheek. A lump was already forming on his temple.

The man across from her leaned forward, pistol steady, eyes cold. "This isn't his fight. It's ours."

Jayda's mind raced, heart battering against her ribs. She swallowed hard, forcing herself upright, though her whole body shook. "I don't want a fight with you," she said quickly, firmly. Her voice surprised her—calm, even. Like she was already in the courtroom, standing before a jury.

The man tilted his head, amused.

Jayda pushed forward. "I was in the wrong place at the wrong time. That's all. I'm a law student. I...I tend to get caught up in the rules. You were breaking the rules—taking that case file out of the library. That's why I reacted." She nodded toward his gun. "I would never have used my stun gun if you hadn't pulled that on me first."

His lips quirked. He was enjoying this.

Her hands trembled, but she clasped them tightly in her lap, steadying her voice. "The papers are gone. I can't give you what you want."

The man's smile vanished. "Oh, you'll give me exactly what I want." He leaned closer, the gun now angled slightly toward Michael's unconscious body. "You're going to lead me straight to my sister."

Jayda's pulse surged. Veronica was his *sister*? Was this how he treated his family? He could take a lesson from the Blairs.

She schooled her face into neutrality, summoning every ounce of training, every courtroom rebuttal she'd practiced in mock trials. "I don't know where she is," she said flatly.

The silence that followed suffocated her, but she kept her expression still, taking slow breaths.

His eyes narrowed.

The muzzle of the gun dipped until it rested directly over Michael.

Jayda's composure fractured. Her body moved before her mind could catch up. She lunged forward, falling over Michael, her arms covering him, her face pressed against his chest. "Fine!" The word ripped from her throat, losing this battle so soon, but she had no other choice. *I'm so sorry, Veronica.* "She's in California. Just leave him alone!"

For a heartbeat, the only sound in the car was Jayda's ragged breathing and the hum of the engine.

"San Fran? I should have known. Our traitorous mother's hometown."

Jayda dropped her gaze, knowing she gave more information away even without saying the city. Some lawyer she would have made.

Then a low chuckle rolled out of the man. Veronica's blood relative, who was out for her blood, leaned back, relaxed again, the pistol shifting its aim back to Jayda. His smile was satisfied, almost tender in its cruelty. "I knew you'd see it my way. Get him out of here."

"No!"

The car slowed, and the second man opened the door just enough to kick Michael to the curb. The door shut before she could see if he was all right. The car took off again, heading up the mountain pass, leaving Michael behind. Jayda could only pray Ginny and Ed would find him in time.

And that they would find her too. Right now, the only place Jayda wanted to be was home with her family.

The first thing Michael felt was cold. The icy wind bit into his skin, stole his breath, and scraped at his lungs. His body ached as if it had been wrung out and discarded, every bone protesting as he stirred from a frozen snowbank. When he opened his eyes, flakes of snow fell onto his lashes, and the world around him was white and spinning. He was lying half on the frozen shoulder of a mountain road, half in a drift, the crunch of distant tires still ringing in his ears.

For a long, heart-stopping second, he couldn't place where he was—or why. Then it all came back in a rush: the black car, the men, Jayda's scream muffled under their grip, his own desperate attempt to shield her before something cracked against his skull.

Jayda.

The word was a shout inside his mind, louder than his pulse.

He pushed himself upright too fast, his head reeling. He staggered, boots slipping on the icy gravel. His hands fumbled for purchase on the guardrail. The car—where was the car? He spun, his gaze sweeping the winding road. The sound of an engine roared faintly in the distance, already climbing higher into the mountains, carrying her farther and farther away.

"Michael!"

The voice hit him through the haze, clear and frantic. A yellow cab skidded to a stop on the icy road, brakes squealing. Out tumbled his father, his overcoat whipping in the wind, and Ginny right behind, clutching her scarf. They were both running to him before he could find his balance, their faces a mixture of fear and relief.

Ginny was the first to reach him, her hands cupping his cheeks, tilting his face this way and that. "Michael—oh, thank God. You're bleeding, your head—you need a doctor."

Ed's hand was firm on his shoulder, steadying him. "Son, can you stand? Did they shoot you?"

"I'm fine," Michael rasped, shrugging them off. His voice was raw, shaking. "It doesn't matter. Jayda—she's still in that car."

He pointed down the mountain road, where the mobsters' vehicle was only a shrinking blur against the white horizon. Panic twisted inside him like a blade. "They've got her. If we don't catch up, they'll kill her."

Ginny grabbed his arm. "We've called the police. Let them handle this. Please, Michael—you're hurt, and those men—"

"No!" His shout echoed off the jagged rocks, sharper than he intended, but he didn't care. He tore free of her grip, chest heaving. "The police won't get to her in time. You saw how fast they're moving. By the time anyone catches up, she'll be gone. I can't—" His voice broke. He closed his eyes, forcing himself to breathe. "I can't let her be alone in this."

For a moment, silence pressed between them, the snowfall filling it with a muffled hush.

Then Ed stepped forward, his gaze steady. "What do you want us to do?"

Michael blinked at him. The question was simple, but it hit deep, because it wasn't just about Jayda. It was about everything—years of strained silences, of him never being sure if he was enough in his father's eyes. And here was Ed, standing in the freezing wind, saying with his presence what he hadn't always said with words: I'm with you.

Michael swallowed hard. His throat felt tight.

"You two have fought for Jayda for years," he said quietly, his eyes flicking between them. "Even when she didn't know it. Even when she didn't want you to." He looked at his father. "I know you pulled strings. Yale Law—that was you, wasn't it? You used your connections. You got her in."

Ed's jaw tightened, his breath clouding in the air. Then he shook his head. "No, son. I told only the truth about her. That girl's one of the hardest workers I've ever seen. Tougher than most of the lawyers I've sat across from. Justice needs people like her. She earned her way." His gaze softened, though his voice didn't. "Just like you earned yours as a writer."

Michael stared at him, chest thick with emotions he hadn't expected. For years he had believed he was living in the shadow of his father's judgments, but here was the man saying he'd seen Michael's worth all along.

His vision blurred for a second, but he blinked it away. There wasn't time for this. "Then don't stop fighting for her now," Michael said, his voice steadier, sharper. "Your gift to her has always been fighting in secret. But she doesn't need secrets anymore. She needs people who'll stand up for her, right in front of her. She needs us."

Ed studied him for a moment, then nodded. "Get in the cab. We've got a mobster to catch."

Ginny's eyes flashed with fear, but she pressed her lips tight and didn't argue. Instead, she grabbed Michael's arm and half-dragged him back toward the cab, as though her own urgency couldn't be denied either.

They piled into the backseat, slamming the doors shut. The cab driver, a wiry man with weathered skin and nerves of steel, had already seen the other car ahead. Without waiting for instructions, he floored the gas pedal, tires spitting snow as they lurched forward into the chase.

Michael's heart thudded, every muscle tight. He leaned forward between the seats, eyes locked on the black car weaving ahead of them far in the distance. Jayda was in there. Somewhere between those tinted windows and steel doors, she was trapped—and counting on him.

"Faster," Michael urged. His pulse kept time with the tires hammering against the icy road. "Don't let them out of sight."

The driver grinned through gritted teeth. "Buckle up. You want me to keep up with those animals, you'd better hang on."

The cab shot forward, sliding dangerously on the next curve, but the driver handled it like he'd been born to these roads. Michael barely noticed. His focus was a burning tunnel on the car ahead, on Jayda.

Then the black car's left rear window slid down.

For one suspended second, nothing moved. Then the muzzle of a gun appeared, gleaming even in the dim light.

"Down!" Michael roared, throwing his arm out across his mother as the first shot cracked through the air.

The windshield splintered with a spiderweb of cracks. Ginny screamed. The cab jerked as the driver swerved, narrowly avoiding the guardrail.

Another shot rang out.

Michael's stomach turned to ice—but his resolve only sharpened.

He would not let up until Jayda was back in his arms.

Fourteen

The limo hurtled through the twisting mountain road, its heavy frame groaning as it swerved tight corners in the Rockies. The windows rattled with the force of the gunfire, glass trembling as one mobster leaned out, firing round after round at the yellow cab barreling behind them. Muzzle flashes lit the night like firecrackers, illuminating the jagged cliffs on one side and the abyss on the other. Snow whipped past the windshield, carried in gusts of icy wind that howled against the metal.

Jayda's pulse pounded like a war drum in her ears. She was pressed against the leather seat, her hands clenched into fists as though they alone might keep her alive. Her voice cracked as she screamed, "You promised to let him go!"

The man beside her didn't even glance at her, too focused on reloading, too smug in the way he tugged back the slide. His partner cackled as he leaned out of the opposite window, bullets spitting fire into the dark. The only good thing was Ginny and Ed had Michael.

Jayda swallowed hard, forcing the rising sob back down. Michael was alive. They had him.

It was the least she could give them, wasn't it? After everything. After years of being taken into their home, only to retreat again and again. She told herself she didn't belong, told herself it was safer to stay away. That Blair house was theirs, never hers. But Ginny never stopped calling. Every Christmas, every summer, Jayda's phone lit up with the same hopeful voice, offering her a place at their table. Offering her family.

And every time, Jayda told them no. She built walls high and thick, pretending she was protecting herself from the moment they discovered she wasn't worth their kindness. But tonight—tonight, on a mountain road lighted with muzzle flashes, she finally saw it clearly. They'd known who she was all along. They knew the runaway, the foster kid who kept one foot out the door, the girl who'd slept on cold concrete floors with gangs who treated her like currency. They knew the worst of her. And they still came for her.

Even now, even when bullets ripped through the night, Ginny and Ed and Michael refused to stop chasing her down.

Jayda's throat tightened. They loved her. No matter how far she ran, no matter how cruelly she'd rejected them, they never stopped waiting. Never stopped fighting.

They were her family.

And suddenly—savagely—Jayda wanted to tell them. To scream it through the snow and the bullets and the roar of the engine: *I love you too. I've been blind. I've been ungrateful. You were right, Michael. You were always right.*

The words stayed trapped inside her chest, burning her from the inside.

The mobster beside her swung his gun around, leveling it at her head. His lips twisted into a sneer. "Don't even think about playing the hero, sweetheart."

Something inside Jayda snapped. Her body remembered what her mind tried to forget—the lessons of survival carved into her bones from years on the street. She moved before fear could lock her down. Her heel shot out in a vicious arc, catching his wrist. The gun went wide as his body jerked to the right, his shout tearing through the air.

Jayda grabbed for the opposite door where the other man was still leaning halfway out, firing into the storm. She shoved it hard, the door swinging open. Snow and wind tore into the cabin, and with a grunt she kicked out, her boot slamming into his back. He toppled, his gun flying into the air as his body tumbled out into the night, disappearing beneath the churn of headlights and ice.

Jayda turned—and froze.

Veronica's brother's mouth curled into a cruel smile as he lunged, rage in every taut line of his face.

"It's just you and me now," he said in a lethal voice, the words like poison.

The driver's silhouette shifted behind the partition, the car jerking as the limo swerved dangerously close to the cliff's edge and back on the road.

The quick momentum caused the man to drop the gun, which clattered to the floor. Both of them dove for it at the same time. Jayda's hand closed over his wrist, his fingers clawing for a grip. She sank her teeth into his knuckles, biting down until the taste of iron filled her mouth. He roared, trying to shake her off, but she held on, fighting with the desperation of a woman who knew there was no second chance.

If he killed her, Veronica was next. He would never stop.

Throughout her whole life, Jayda thought justice lived in courtrooms, in clean suits and closing arguments. She wanted to be that lawyer—the one who fought for women like Veronica, women like her mother. But here, in this moment, she understood: sometimes justice wasn't words. Sometimes it was survival. Sometimes it was a fight to the death in the back of a limo speeding toward a cliff.

The car jolted again. But this time, metal screamed as another vehicle slammed into their bumper. The impact hurled Jayda forward, slamming her shoulder into the partition. The mobster's fist cracked against her jaw as they both reached again for the gun.

The weapon went off with a thunderous bang. The bullet punched through the glass divider, shattering it into a spiderweb of shards. The driver screamed.

Through the fractured glass, Jayda saw his door burst open. He hurled himself into the snow, rolling out of sight.

The wheel jerked. The limo careened wildly, the headlights casting dizzy arcs across the cliffside.

The mobster's eyes glowed with manic triumph as his hand finally closed around the grip of the gun. He twisted it up, pressing the barrel to her chest.

Jayda didn't think—she reached for the door handle, shoving the door open against the force of the wind.

The car tilted, nose sliding toward the abyss.

The man laughed, the sound raw and jagged. "End of the road."

The gunshot cracked like lightning as the limo pitched forward.

Jayda hurled herself out, the icy wind ripping the breath from her lungs as the bullet ripped through her side. Snow exploded around her as she hit the ground, tumbling to the edge of the cliff. Her body screamed in pain, her vision tunneled to black at the edges.

Far behind, the limo's frame shrieked as it tore through the guardrail, the last crash echoing as it plunged into the darkness below.

Jayda lay in the snow, her body convulsing. Warmth spread across her side where the bullet had grazed her, the blood seeping hot against the icy powder. Her limbs felt too heavy to move, her breath hitching in shallow gasps.

Voices shouted in the distance. Tires skidded.

And then—Michael. His voice. Desperate, breaking, calling her name.

Jayda wanted to tell him. She wanted to tell him he'd been right, that she loved him, that she was done running. Her lips parted, but no sound came out.

Strong arms scooped her from the snow, pulling her against a chest she knew as well as her own heartbeat. Michael. She pressed her face into him, the scent of snow and blood and his cologne mingling in her fading awareness.

Safe. She was safe.

She welcomed the darkness as it surged up and swallowed her whole.

Michael cradled Jayda against his chest, the frigid mountain air burning in his lungs with every shaky breath. Her body felt too limp, too light, as though she'd poured out everything she had left in that desperate escape from the limo. Her blood stained the snow beneath them, but her chest rose, shallow and uneven, proof of life.

"Hold on, Jayda," he whispered fiercely, his lips pressed against her hair. He hadn't even realized the tears slipping hot down his face until they froze on his cheeks. "I've got you. You're safe."

Sirens wailed faintly in the distance, growing louder. A paramedic team skidded to a stop near the cliff's edge. Snow churned under boots as the medics rushed toward them, shouting for space. Michael didn't want to let her go, not even when the paramedics pried her gently from his arms to check vitals, sliding oxygen beneath her nose.

Ginny gently pulled him away, fussing over him in

nervousness. But she froze when Jayda's eyelashes fluttered open.

Jayda's groggy voice cracked through the night. "M-Michael?"

Michael almost collapsed right there. Relief ripped through him so hard he swayed, pressing a fist to his mouth to hold back the sob threatening to spill. He hadn't realized how tightly fear had coiled inside him until he heard her voice call to him.

"She's okay," he whispered, to no one, to everyone. "She's okay. I'm here, Jayda. Let the paramedics help you."

Ed's voice cut through the air, low and steady, carrying that courtroom authority that could silence a storm. Michael looked up to see his father half-dragging, half-shoving a bloodied man toward the waiting deputies. The shooter Jayda had kicked from the car. His face was mangled, his limp was heavy, his eyes wild with pain and rage.

Ed's grip didn't waver. He thrust the man forward. "This one messed with the wrong family." His jaw was hard as steel, his gaze unflinching. "With a lawyer and a judge in this family, he won't see daylight again."

Michael's chest swelled. The words didn't feel like lines from a closing argument. They felt like a vow.

Jayda's lips trembled as fresh tears cut through the dirt on her cheeks. "I—I didn't take my final," she rasped, as though this was the crime that mattered most. "I'll fail the class. Yale won't give me another shot."

Michael shook his head, half laughing at the absurdity of her worrying about exams when she'd just survived a mob war on a cliffside. But before he could answer, Ed crouched beside her, his voice steady.

"Circumstances matter, Jayda," he said, his eyes softening. "Taking down a mob boss in the Rockies may just earn you bonus points."

Michael caught the twitch in his father's jaw, the way his mouth stopped just shy of offering more—just shy of promising to make a call. The old accusation hovered like smoke between them, that his father had pulled strings to get Jayda into Yale.

But for the first time, Michael saw the truth clearly. His father didn't cheat for her. He just told the truth—about who she was, how hard she fought, how worthy she'd always been.

And maybe it was time someone boasted about her.

Michael's throat burned. He met his father's eyes. "Couldn't you make a call?"

Ed's eyebrows lifted. "You're sure about that?"

Michael nodded, his voice firm. "It's what you do for family. You show up. You lift them up when they can't do it themselves."

For a moment, silence hung heavy and raw. Then Ed's mouth curved—not into his polished courtroom smile but into something rarer. Pride. Pure and unguarded.

Michael felt it like sunlight through his veins.

Jayda's lips parted, her voice hoarse. "I can't accept—"

"No." Three voices cut her off at once—Michael's, Ginny's, Ed's. The force of it made her blink, startled.

Ginny's eyes shone with tears. Ed's hand rested on her shoulder. Michael leaned down until their foreheads nearly touched.

"You don't get to push your family away anymore," he said firmly.

Jayda stared at them, wide-eyed. Then, unexpectedly, she laughed. The sound was broken, jagged, and it split her lip wider, blood spotting her teeth. She winced, hissing through clenched teeth.

Michael was already there, brushing his thumb tenderly across her mouth, pressing a feather-light kiss to the hurt. "Easy," he whispered.

Her smirk curved carefully. "Care to make that...legal?"

Michael barked a laugh, the sound tumbling out raw with disbelief and joy. "Why am I not surprised Jayda Simone would be the one to propose? You always had to be first at everything."

Ginny gasped, her hands flying to her mouth before clapping together like a child's. "Hurry and say yes, Michael!"

Michael grinned down at Jayda, his heart so full it hurt. "Yes," he said, voice steady, strong. "But don't make me wait too long."

Ed cleared his throat, his arm sliding around Ginny's waist. "I do happen to be a judge," he said, dry and deliberate. "In case you forgot."

Michael's eyes widened, flicking to Jayda's. "How about Christmas Eve?" he asked, his voice suddenly thick and nervous. "At home."

Jayda's eyes filled with tears, spilling freely. She nodded, whispering, "Home is the perfect place."

Michael sealed their pledge with a kiss, blood and salt and snow between them, but none of it mattered. In just a few days, they would be husband and wife, and Jayda would finally be a Blair.

Epilogue

Jayda stood at the end of her old four-poster bed, draped in soft linens with the same quilt folded neatly across the footboard and the same window that overlooked the snow-blanketed lawn below. As a teenager, she had walked the fine line between guest and almost-daughter, grateful for Ginny's open arms but always keeping her heart at arm's length. Tonight, though, it didn't feel like she was borrowing a place to sleep. Tonight, she was home.

Her reflection in the mirror startled her. The white winter velvet dress hugged her frame, elegant yet simple, the hem brushing her ankles. It wasn't anything flashy. She didn't want glitter or lace. Her pink bedazzled stun gun proved glitz didn't make her strong. Velvet felt solid and warm, and for the first time in years, she saw not just the survivor or the street-smart girl who had fought her way through too many battles. She saw a warrior bride.

Michael's bride.

It took her far too long to realize her mother would have been happy for her, happy to see her in this house, embraced by a family that refused to let her go, and loved by a man she could trust with her life. For so long, Jayda had carried guilt, believing her mother's struggles meant Jayda had no right to find her place to belong. But she forgot that was what her mother had fought so hard for—a home for her daughter.

A soft knock pulled her from her thoughts. Her heart jumped.

She cracked the door open an inch. Michael stood there, tall and ridiculously handsome in his dark suit. His tie was slightly crooked, his hair tousled as though he'd been running his hands through it since the moment they'd parted. His beautiful blue eyes warmed when they found hers.

"You can't see me," she whispered through the slit. "Not before the ceremony."

His grin was pure trouble. "Then this'll have to be quick." He leaned down and stole a kiss through the narrow opening, his lips brushing hers, sending heat curling all the way to her toes.

"Michael," she warned, breathless.

"You're missing something," he said. His hand slipped into his pocket and came back with a small, timeworn box.

Her breath caught. "Another gift?"

"Another? What other gift have I given you?"

"Too many to count," she said in all seriousness.

He smiled. "Have I told you I love you?" he said and opened the box to reveal a diamond ring inside. The breathtaking solitaire with an old-world cut, set in platinum, looked to have weathered time without losing its strength. Michael's eyes glistened as he continued, "This belonged to my grandmother. She'd be so happy to see it on you."

Jayda pulled the door wider, her hand flying to her mouth. "Michael..." Jayda traced the cool metal, humbled. "I wish I had known her personally. But her gift...I'll always cherish it."

"You already honor her," Michael said, his voice catching. "You honor all of us."

He took her hand gently, sliding the ring onto her finger as though it had always belonged there. "Now it's official," he murmured, his gaze locked on hers. "And in a few minutes, we'll make it forever."

Her throat thickened. She glanced at the ring, then back at him. "Did you—did you turn in your article?"

Another grin tugged at his lips. "Wrote it on the flight back from Denver. Harold loved it."

She shook her head in disbelief. "Of course he did."

"He especially loved the part about secret gifts. We never made it to San Francisco," he said in a hushed voice, brushing his thumb along her knuckles. "But your mission of protecting Veronica in secret was an amazing gift." His voice lowered, reverent. "She'll never know how fiercely you fought for her."

Jayda's chest squeezed. "Guess that makes me a true Blair. A real fighter."

"Always were."

She swallowed hard, then managed a shaky smile. "I can't wait to read your article in the morning. Even though I already know it'll be fabulous."

"I hope others like it as much as I loved writing it." His grin turned rueful. "I think I managed to capture the Christmas spirit my editor wanted. Even if the tinsel and bells were swapped out for guns and whistles."

A laugh bubbled out of her, and she covered her mouth. "Now, I'm intrigued. Tell me more."

"The joy of giving came through," he added. His voice softened. "Especially the gift of forgiving." His gaze searched hers, full of trust and love. "I've never felt so free, Jayda, as I do since you forgave me for my past mistakes."

Her eyes stung. She opened her mouth, but before she could answer, Ginny's voice rang up from the bottom of the stairs.

"Michael Blair! Get away from that door. It's bad luck to see the bride before the wedding!"

Jayda bit back a laugh, pressing a hand to her lips.

Ed's heavy footsteps sounded on the stairs. A moment later, his voice joined his wife's, dry but commanding. "Son, step aside. She's not your wife until I give her away."

Michael's mouth quirked, but he straightened obediently. "Yes, sir."

And then, because he could never leave well enough alone, he leaned in through the gap, cupped Jayda's face, and kissed her until her knees weakened. It wasn't a polite brush this time—it was a promise, one that curled her toes and sent her heart thundering.

"I love you, Michael," Jayda whispered. "I can't wait to spend the rest of my life getting into trouble with you."

He rested his forehead against hers. "I'll meet you under the mistletoe." His breath fanned her lips. "And then no one will ever tear us apart again."

"Promise?"

"Just let them try."

Her smile trembled. Her entire body tingled. She was going to love being married to this man.

He slipped away down the hall, his steps light, his laughter echoing.

Ed appeared in the doorway, his broad frame filling the space. His eyes softened as they met hers. He offered his arm, formal and tender all at once. "Are you ready to become a Blair?"

Jayda's pulse thrummed in her ears. She glanced back once at the room, the quilt, the window. The place that had once felt like borrowed space now felt wholly hers.

She stepped forward, velvet brushing her ankles, her chin lifting with newfound certainty.

Sliding her hand into Ed's arm, she smiled, sure and

unshakable. "I was born ready. I'm just sorry it took me so long to realize it."

Ed's answering smile held both pride and forgiveness. Together, they turned toward the staircase, toward the glow of candlelight and the waiting vows, toward the family that had never stopped fighting for her.

And Jayda knew without a doubt that she was finally home.

Afterword

Dear Reader,

I hope you enjoyed this wild cross-country Christmas train ride with Michael and Jayda. If you enjoy a little humor in your romantic suspense, check out *Real Cold* from the Web of Lies series.

But what started as a simple "what if" turned into a cross-country journey I didn't expect. What if one moment changed everything? What if running felt safer than staying? And what if the very place you swore you didn't belong...was the only place you were ever truly meant to be? Jayda Simone's story came to life as my own adopted daughter became an adult and chose us to be her family for life. Just like my own daughter, Jayda was a fighter, shaped by loss, independence, and a fierce determination to never need anyone. But as danger closed in, she was forced to confront a truth many of us wrestle with: we weren't created to do life alone. This story is about more than a train ride, a chase, or even a romance. It's about family—the kind we're born into, and the kind we choose. It's about grace that keeps showing up, even when we push it away. And it's about risking everything for love. As you turned these pages, I hope you felt the rush of the chase, the warmth of unexpected laughter, and the quiet pull of a place called home. My prayer is that you'll be reminded that no matter how far you've run, you are never beyond the reach of love.

And get this! This journey doesn't end on the page. Jayda and Michael's story is also coming to life in a new way—as a vertical film experience, designed to be watched one episode at a time, right on your phone in the palm of your hand. It's fast, emotional, suspenseful, and full of the same heart you've just experienced here. Be watching for it. You won't want to miss seeing these moments unfold in motion.

Thank you for taking this journey with me. I'm so glad you're here.

With gratitude,

Katy Lee
Katy@KatyLeeBooks.com
https://www.katyleebooks.com/

About Katy Lee

#1 Publishers Weekly Bestselling Author Katy Lee has published more than 40 novels, including her Harlequin Love Inspired Suspense books. She writes inspiring stories filled with high speed suspense and sweet romance. Katy has multiple awards and nominations, including Romance Writers of America's RITA® Awards, the Daphne du Maurier Mystery Awards, the Faith, Hope, & Love's Inspirational Reader's Choice Awards, and Selah Awards. Katy also teaches and coaches new and seasoned writers online and at her week-long writing retreats. She runs a literary non-profit organization for guiding people to heal through writing called Story Haven Writers, Inc. Katy lives in the rugged mountains of Utah and is a special education teacher when she's not plotting her next story.

Interact with Katy Lee at:

Website: http://www.katyleebooks.com/
Katy's Writing Masterclass: https://buymeacoffee.com/storyhavenwriters

amazon.com/author/katylee
facebook.com/KatyLeewriter
instagram.com/katyleeauthor
bookbub.com/profile/katy-lee
youtube.com/@KatyLeeBooks

Also by Katy Lee

Other Katy Lee Book Titles:

Table for One

Left at the altar may just be the best thing that's ever happened to her.

Becca Shane has a cruise to catch, even if she is now boarding her honeymoon solo.

Patrick Joyce has a daughter to raise after his wife turned her back on him when he needed her the most.

Neither believe in love, but can they believe in each other?

A short-story prequel to the Royal Bay Beach Billionaires series

Free when you subscribe to Katy's Novel Ideas Newsletter here: https://BookHip.com/QLBXZBF

Or buy on Amazon: https://amzn.to/47eN7to

Two Wrongs to Right

Rubi Stone is a single mom who is navigating her recent widowhood as she keeps her charter boat business afloat in Royal Bay. Grady Andrews is only interested in taking down the billionaire tycoon who runs the seaside town and figures the locals will thank him for it in the end, even if they don't realize it yet. With his plan set to destroy the beach club from the inside, all that's stopping him is his growing concern for Captain Rubi and her little girl. His actions could send them both adrift in the storm he's creating. But could Rubi's love be the lifesaver he needs to set him on the right path...and into her arms forever?

Royal Bay Beach Club series

Buy Now.

Three Fine Days

(Coming Soon)

Four Warned

(Coming Soon)

Real Virtue

***Real Virtue* blends fast-paced suspense, sweet romance with the thrill of an online world turned deadly.**

Mel Mesini has built a successful life far from the small town that once branded her an outcast. When her father is the victim of a hit-and-run, Mel's forced back into the one place she vowed never to return—and directly into the path of the man whose rejection stung the most—Police Officer Jeremy Stiles.

Jeremy has spent years regretting how he had driven Mel away and wants to make things right. He sees a chance by finding her father's assailant—until his investigation opens a door to a dangerous world that Mel is involved in. As a hidden predator closes in, time is ticking for Mel and Jeremy to reunite and fight for their second chance.

Will a killer tear them apart forever? Or will their love win them the future they were always meant to have?

Buy Now.

Real Justice

A ransom note left in her apartment tells Christina Depalo that changing her name and hiding in the big city hadn't been enough to escape her dangerous family. The Morans have kidnapped her roommate, demanding Christina return to Georgia. But that will mean facing the cutthroat attorney Marcus Cartwright, a man she once loved but who only wanted to take down her family.

Marcus had started a coalition with his friend to crack down on organized crime in Savannah. But when his friend loses his life in a supposed accident, nothing will stop Marcus from seeking justice, not even the Moran's prodigal daughter who left town twelve years ago. Nobody will derail him this time.

But then Christina never was a nobody.

Buy Now.

Real Cold

FBI agent Vera Sharp needs to close in on a dangerous crime lord before he carries out his most lethal heist yet. She'll go undercover as a singer to get her man.

Chef Rafe Sinclair's restaurant is on it lasts breath and he wonders if he's being sabotaged. When his newest singer turns out to be investigating him as a criminal, he knows he's also being setup. With Rafe's colorful past, he'll have to prove himself innocent to the powerful and stunning agent.

Vera always gets her man, but this time she may be all wrong about the right man—for her.

Buy Now.

Warning Signs

GUILTY UNTIL PROVEN INNOCENT

When a drug-smuggling ring rocks a small coastal town, the DEA sends Agent Owen Matthews to shut it down. A single father with a deaf son, Owen senses that the town's number one suspect—the high school's new principal—doesn't fit the profile. Miriam Hunter hoped to shrug off the stigma of her hearing impairment when she returned to Stepping Stones, Maine. But her recurring nightmares dredge up old memories that could prove her innocence—and uncover the truth behind a decades-old murder. Yet Owen's help may not be enough when someone decides to keep Miriam silenced—permanently.

Stepping Stones Island Series Book 1

Buy Now.

Grave Danger

BONES OF CONTENTION

When skeletal remains are found on a small Maine island, forensic anthropologist Lydia Muir is sent to investigate. It's Lydia's job to determine whether the homicide happened long ago—or more recently. Island sheriff Wesley Grant seems sure the murder didn't happen on *his* watch. But when Lydia uncovers the victim's identity, someone goes to great lengths to get Lydia off the island. Wes vows to protect her, but is the handsome lawman holding something back? To help catch a killer, she'll have to trust him—or become the next victim.

Stepping Stones Island series Book 2

Buy Now.

Sunken Treasure

DANGER ON THE HIGH SEAS

Shipwreck diver Gage Fontaine is used to modern-day pirates chasing after his boat and the buried treasure he salvages. But when he unknowingly leads a dangerous criminal to the waters off Stepping Stones Island, he puts a beautiful fisherwoman in grave danger. Rachelle Thibodaux has spent the past year hiding on her boat to avoid the town's censure for her father's crimes. But when she comes face-to-face with a gun-wielding pirate, she becomes a new kind of target. To save her own life, she'll have to work with Gage to find the treasure before the pirates do.

Stepping Stones Island Series Book 3

Buy Now.

Permanent Vacancy

BUYER BEWARE

When Gretchen Bauer begins renovating an old Victorian house to turn it into a bed-and-breakfast, she barely escapes several dangerous "accidents" at her home. Colm McCrae, host of the home improvement TV show helping her renovate, refuses to believe these aren't on purpose. Could this be a harmful ploy by his boss to boost ratings? Yet with Colm's Irish brogue and handsome face, Gretchen wonders whether he could be involved. But with a whole town full of neighbors disgruntled about the inn bringing strangers to their shores, Gretchen has a list of more likely suspects. Now she must trust Colm if she wants to keep her new business venture from turning into a five-star death trap.

Stepping Stones Island Series Book 4

Buy Now.

Silent Night Pursuit

RACE AGAINST TIME

Lacey Phillips believes Captain Wade Spencer knows something about her brother's mysterious death. So she throws caution to the wind and tracks him down on Christmas Eve looking for answers. Wade tries to turn her away—until bullets start to fly. He doesn't want to take the stubborn beauty on his life-or-death mission to find out the truth about how Wade's past may have cost her brother his life. But with killers lurking everywhere, he has to protect her—especially when she breaches the walls around his heart. Can Wade and his faithful service dog keep Lacey alive long enough to figure out who's targeting them?

Roads to Danger Series Book 1: Family secrets resurface

Buy Now.

Ransom Rescue (previously Blindsided)

When race-car track owner Veronica Spencer discovers stolen cars in a garage on her track, she knows she's been framed. But before Roni can do anything about it, the criminals kidnap her. Undercover FBI agent Ethan Gunn shouldn't break his cover to protect Roni, but he won't watch her die, either. Despite his FBI information that says she's involved in the crime ring, Ethan knows she's innocent. So he risks it all to help her break free. But now, with killers and the FBI on their trail, Ethan must find a way to keep her safe...and clear her name.

Roads to Danger Series Book 2: Family secrets resurface

Buy Now.

High Speed Holiday

After Ian Stone discovers he was kidnapped when he was a baby, he journeys to his "family's" hometown—and is shot at shortly after he arrives. Now he's convinced the Spencers don't want their long-lost brother, Luke, to return and claim his inheritance. But local chief of police Sylvie Laurent doesn't believe his siblings would try to kill him. And the stubborn woman is determined to protect him until she uncovers the truth. At first, Sylvie is skeptical of Ian's story...but he bears a strong resemblance to the Spencers. And they'll have to work together to stay ahead of the danger if they want to live to see him reunited with his family at Christmas.

Roads to Danger Series Book 3: Family secrets resurface

Buy Now.

Amish Country Undercover

Secrets, sabotage and small-town danger. *Someone wants an Amish woman dead.*

Taking the reins of her father's Amish horse-trading business, Grace Miller's prepared for backlash over breaking community norms—but not for sabotage. Now someone's willing to do anything it takes to make sure she fails, and it's undercover FBI agent Jack Kaufman's mission to stop them. But can Jack face his own Amish past long enough to shield Grace from a killer?

A Rogues Ridge Setting

Buy Now.

Amish Sanctuary

A woman on the run. A baby in danger. Can her Amish ex-fiancé save them?

To keep her patient's baby safe from a killer, counselor Naomi Kemp will do things she never thought possible, like return to her Amish hometown...and her ex-fiancé. Widower Sawyer Zook can offer Naomi and the baby protection and a place to hide. But Sawyer can't shield Naomi from what threatens her most: the traumatic past that drove her away years ago...

A Rogues Ridge Setting

Buy Now.

Framed in Amish Country: A Novella

Despite the disapproval of her Amish community, teacher Lizzie Fisher has fought for an independent life—even going so far as to tutor at the English school. Alex Wilson, a young English painter hired to paint the school, is used to being ridiculed because of his learning disabilities. He questions why the smart, pretty, Amish woman treats him differently. When Alex finds himself framed for a crime, he believes there is no hope for him, but Lizzie is sure her community will come to his aid. Except, their forbidden relationship may give Lizzie the independence she thought she always wanted.

A Rogues Ridge Setting

Buy Now.

Holiday Suspect Pursuit

Unraveling a murder mystery...could unlock his lost memories...

After a murderer strikes, former deputy Jett Butler and his search-and-rescue dog must work with the sole witness—FBI agent Nicole Harrington. But Nicole's the ex-fiancée he left behind after a car accident gave him amnesia years ago. And in a fight to survive the holidays, remembering his past might be just as dangerous as facing the killer on their heels...

Danger in New Mexico Series Book 1

Buy Now.

Cavern Cover Up

In this inspirational Christian romantic suspense, a pretty PI teams up with a handsome park ranger to pursue a dangerous criminal.

Suspecting her father's murder is linked to a smuggling ring sends private investigator Danika Lewis pursuing a lead all the way to Carlsbad Caverns National Park. Teaming up with ranger Tru Butler to search the off-limits caves for the missing artifacts is the fastest way to uncover the truth. But there's danger in the dark and a killer who will do anything to keep secrets hidden.

Danger in New Mexico Series Book 2

Buy Now.

Santa Fe Setup

An artist is caught in the world of drug smuggling—and in a criminal's crosshairs—in this inspirational and suspenseful romance.

After artist Luci Butler discovers someone has been hiding drugs in her paintings, she also finds ruthless killers are aiming to silence her. Only her brother's coworker Bard Holland is on her side. Now they must race to clear her name and track a murderer into unforgiving New Mexico mountains. But Bard's determined protection is drawing Luci dangerously close . . . and into a killer's merciless endgame.

Danger in New Mexico Series Book 2

Buy Now.

Christmas K-9 Unit Heroes

Danger comes to Denver for the holidays...

in these thrilling Rocky Mountain K-9 Unit novellas.

With veterinarian Sydney Jones being targeted, K-9 Officer Gavin

Walker and his furry partner must stand between her and certain death in Lenora Worth's *Hidden Christmas Danger*. And the clock is ticking in *Silent Night Explosion* by Katy Lee—but can Jodie Chen trust the newest K-9 officer, Victor Abrams, and his dog to find a bomb *and* keep her alive...despite Victor's shadowed past?

Christmas K-9 Novellas

Buy Now.

K-9 National Park Defenders

Peril at Christmas awaits... in these gripping Pacific Northwest K-9 Unit novellas

A Christmas skiing retreat turns treacherous when Pacific Northwest K-9 Unit officer Veronica Eastwood's sister is kidnapped—and only rival officer Parker Walsh can help her in Katy Lee's *Yuletide Ransom*.And in Sharee Stover's explosive *Holiday Rescue Countdown*, K-9 officers Dylan Jeong and Brandie Weller must race against the clock when they face a Christmas parade bomb threat...and a killer from Dylan's past.

Christmas K-9 Novellas

Buy Now.

Christmas K-9 Guardians

Christmas in the mountains turns menacing...

in these two exciting Mountain Country K-9 Unit novellas

Protecting a K-9 who's being targeted by a sinister cartel sends veterinarian Michael Tanner and tech analyst Isla Jimenez on the run for their lives in Lenora Worth's *Perilous Christmas Pursuit*. Only, Michael's dangerous secrets are a holiday surprise Isla won't see coming. And in Katy Lee's *Lethal Holiday Hideout*, FBI agent and K-9 officer Cara Haines's life is threatened when her sister's identity in witness protection is compromised. Now she and her ex, US Marshal Sully Briggs, must survive the icy wilderness and assassins before this Christmas becomes their last...

Christmas K-9 Novellas

Buy Now.

Tracing a Kidnapper's Trail

Solving an abduction case means a relentless K-9 manhunt...

When search and rescue worker Hunter Shelton and his bloodhound Libby are called to a crime scene, he discovers his ex-fiancée murdered and her young daughter missing—and he's attacked. Soon, he realizes the little girl may have been taken by drug runners, and could possibly be his own child. With no one else to turn to, Hunter teams up with DEA Agent Marlee Price and her narcotics K-9, despite their rocky history. As they face escalating threats and uncover a rising body count, an old enemy from Marlee's past resurfaces. Will they be able to rescue the child and bring dangerous criminals to justice before time runs out?

Search and Rescue series

Buy Now.

Amish Country Disappearance (LIS)

(Coming January 2027)

Annie's Fiction Books: Sweet contemporary romances and mysteries

Two Birds with One Scone

Hot Cross Burglary

Noel Way Out

Best Laid Plants

One Simple Wish

A Promise to Honor

A Noble Bond

Remote Danger

Harbored Hearts

A Safe Haven

Lucky's Beach

Beneath the Current

www.ingramcontent.com/pod-product-compliance
Lightning Source LLC
LaVergne TN
LVHW041249110826
845146LV00004BA/1262

* 9 7 9 8 9 9 3 5 8 0 1 5 9 *